I'm Fine,
But You
Appear
to Be
Sinking

STORIES BY LEYNA KROW

I'm Fine, But You Appear to Be Sinking

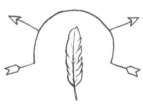

*fe*ather*proof* BOOKS

Versions of the following stories have previously been published: "I'm Fine, But You Appear to Be Sinking" in *Santa Monica Review*; "Tiger, Tiger" in *Sou'wester*; "End Times" in *Ninth Letter*; "Katie Eats Boston Cream Pie at A Motel Diner in Southeast Portland" in *South Dakota Review*; "Habitat" in *The Southeast Review*; "Excitable Creatures" in *Southern Indiana Review*; "Disruption" in *Hayden's Ferry Review*.

Published by
*f*eatherpro*of* books
Chicago, Illinois
www.*f*eatherpro*of*.com

First edition
∞

Library of Congress Control Number: 2016951498
ISBN 13: 978-1943888085

Edited by Jason Sommer and Naomi Huffman
Design by Zach Dodson
Proofread by Sam Axelrod

Set in Baskerville

Printed in the United States of America

For my mom, and my dad

Table of Contents

Index of Things to Come

I'm Fine, But You Appear to Be Sinking

From the notebook of Captain C.J. Wyle, February 1

It's just me, Gideon, and Plymouth now.

Strangely, the Artemis seems smaller with only the three of us onboard. At ten people, our 112-foot trimaran felt spacious, with plenty of room for everyone to go about their respective tasks. There was a constant human hum, but we weren't on top of each other.

Now Gideon and I can't seem to escape ourselves and Plymouth is always under foot. His barking echoes through the narrow hatchways. Shrunken— that's how this whole arrangement feels.

The Pacific Ocean, however, is the same size it's always been.

I don't want to admit anxiety or desperation. That seems unprofessional. But if the boat has moved in recent days, it has been by its own accord and certainly not in any productive direction. We lack the necessary manpower and know-how. I try not to blame Gideon for this. He is, after all, only an intern.

So far, I've managed to avoid making hasty decisions. Inaction, for the time being, seems the safest course of action. The trip has been so marred already by the pitfall of optimism.

When the others started making their preparations, the clouds were high. By the time they had descended and darkened, the inflatable skiff, Righteous Fury, had already been lowered off the stern of the Artemis and into the sea. The protest banners were unfurled and the megaphone batteries charged. It occurs to me now that reasonable men with reasonable aims would have called for a rain check. That's the problem with radicals—they rarely take weather into account.

Gideon had been left behind to keep watch. Together, we observed from the bow as the skiff containing our eight crewmates set off after a whaling ship of unknown nationality. Gideon held a digital video camera. His face was a wide grin.

"Civil disobedience is the highest form of civic participation," he informed me.

I asked whether the maxim still applied in ungovernable waters where there is no civil or civic anything to speak of. Gideon shook his head and told me that right and wrong transcend international boundaries.

The whaling ship had been spotted near the horizon that morning by Gideon himself. It was the first encounter of the trip and the crew's excitement was palpable. I watched as they readied themselves, speaking hurriedly, faces flushed. They knew how to say, "You are in violation of the Endangered Species Act and International Whaling Convention" in thirteen languages. A few had worked out phrases of their own such as, "How would you like to be harpooned?" and, "Every humpback is someone's child." Though technically it would be more accurate to say, "Every humpback is someone's calf," but I suppose that doesn't have quite the same ring.

If the banner waving and slogan shouting did not convince the whalers to turn back, I'd been told by certain crew members that they were prepared to board the rogue vessel. No one would say what might happen once they were inside.

Did this necessity ever come to pass? We'll never know. The skiff was not yet in shouting distance of the whalers when the sky, already gray and noisy, closed in on us, obstructing our view of the only other souls Gideon or I knew in the entire hemisphere. For the next five hours, we were no more than a buoy, bobbing alone in the sputtering froth of warm rain and salty wind.

When the clouds lifted, the whaling vessel was gone from the horizon and so was the skiff Righteous Fury.

It should be noted that the day of the storm, it was Nelson's turn in the galley. Gideon and I were unable to reach an amicable agreement as to who should pick up the slack and make dinner. And so we simply went without eating.

Now, I have designated Gideon as the all-time breadwinner, and baker (if I may be so bold as to extend the analogy). There are plenty of canned goods in the galley, but the supply is certainly not infinite. I suggested we ought to supplement these items with fresh fish. This part of the ocean is rich with life, after all. Gideon was not initially pleased with the idea, claiming he is an ultra-strict vegan and refuses to eat anything that casts a shadow. I told him this was no excuse for shirking his responsibility to the remaining crewmembers, myself and Plymouth specifically, but he insisted. So I've had to find other ways of motivating him.

"Gideon," I say when I get hungry, "catch me some fish, or I'm going to kill your dog and eat it." He practically jumps for his pole every time.

The same threat works for getting other tasks done as well.

"Gideon, straighten the lines, or I'll kill your dog and eat it." "Gideon, empty the bilge, or I'll kill your dog and eat it." "Gideon, bring me the binoculars…" You get the idea.

Unfortunately, this ploy may have a limited lifespan. Gideon has already succeeded in hiding almost all the knives onboard and has begun removing cleats and other metal affixtures from the deck for good measure.

From the notebook of Captain C.J. Wyle, February 4

There's been no wind for days, as if the ocean wore itself out swallowing our comrades. I lick my lips and feel nothing against them. It's almost a relief. I know my limitations.

I wish I could say the same for my shipmates.

Gideon paces the deck in the heat of the afternoon, Plymouth always nearby. He fiddles with ropes and cranks and looks expectantly toward the sky and then down into the water. He wants to know what we are going to do.

I keep telling him there are Quaaludes in my toiletries kit and grain alcohol in the galley and we can worry about further logistics once those are gone. He finds this answer unsatisfying.

From the notebook of Captain C.J. Wyle, February 5

At noon, Gideon called to me, saying I should come up top with him to look at the octopus. But I stayed put. I've seen the octopus before and what's more, as I've already told Gideon, it's not an octopus. It's a giant squid. Octopuses don't get that large.

Gideon believes it's an omen, a harbinger of good luck. We first saw it the day after the storm—a shimmering, near-translucent mass passing beneath us. It was gone in an instant, but the goose bumps on my arms lingered for half an hour. Now, the squid stays longer, hovering under the Artemis, doing God knows what.

Gideon thinks the creature has come to comfort us in our time of loss. I think it's stalking us. It senses our weakness and is biding its time.

I hear its tentacles pressing against the hull at night. Suction cups attaching and releasing, toying with its prey until the right moment. It would eat us whole in the crunchy wrapping of our fiberglass boat if it could.

From the notebook of Captain C.J. Wyle, February 7

It should be known that I am not Captain C.J. Wyle.

True, this is his journal. But I commandeered it after the storm, ripped out his notes on the trip thus far (going well, he felt), and dropped them overboard in hopes that they might meet up with their original owner.

It's not that I don't have notebooks of my own. I do. And pens, and a camera, and a digital voice recording device—all the necessary tools for a member of the fourth estate.

My assignment, for *Popular Anarchist Quarterly*, was to accompany the team from a newly formed oceanic protection agency (as they like to be called) on their maiden voyage. The organization, operating under the handle Save Our Sea Mammals, or SOSM, is in its infancy, but its organizers are hardly unknowns in the world of nautical activism. In fact, just last year, I did a profile on SOSM founder Erica Luntz for her work in various West Coast ports of call sabotaging naval icebreakers bound for the North Pole. These boats, it seems, present a terrible danger to both polar bears and their adorable prey.

The story was a hit with *Popular Anarchist* readers and my editors were keen for a follow-up with Luntz on her newest venture. For five weeks of embedded reporting, I was promised the cover and an eight-page spread.

Does this seem like a lot to go through for top billing in a niche magazine? Perhaps. But let me assure you, *Popular Anarchist* is the premier journal for radical discourse. It's a thoughtful publication. No syndicalist screeds or dirty bomb recipes to be found in its pages. Rather, it promotes a more moderate approach for smashing the state.

So this is kind of a big break for me. Especially because—I'll be the first to admit—I am not a very good reporter. I have a tendency to sacrifice accuracy for style. I'd rather write something that sounds good than something that's true. I never lie. But I do embellish. For example, whenever I am writing about a group of people coming together for any purpose, I always like to say, "a crowd gathered," no matter how many people there really were, crowd-like or not.

I hope you can see then why I might want to keep a record of these events separate from my work. It's a matter of clarity and veracity.

From the notebook of Captain C.J. Wyle, February 8

Around noon, a crowd gathered at the stern. Someone had spotted something. Gideon, Plymouth, and I stared out at a single blemish in the otherwise unmarred blue of the stupid endless sky. The blemish appeared to be moving toward us.

"It's a plane," Gideon said with the real excitement of someone who really believes he's looking at a real airplane.

He took off his bright yellow SOSM t-shirt and waved it above his head.

I looked up at the thing, silent and encased in atmosphere. Even far away it was too small to be a plane.

"It's only a bird," I said. "Probably an albatross."

"No. There's no such thing as an albatross," Gideon countered, still whipping his shirt around. "They're just something Disney made up for that movie about the mice who go to Australia."

"You're thinking of pterodactyls," I said. "And *The Land Before Time* wasn't a Disney film. It was Spielberg."

"Pterodactyls? No, you're thinking of mastodons. And that's not even the right movie anyway."

"A mastodon doesn't fly," I corrected. "It's like a woolly mammoth. There's no way *that* is a mastodon."

I pointed to the object in the sky for emphasis, but it was gone.

From the notebook of Captain C.J. Wyle, February 9

This has to be the sleepiest dog on Earth. Or at least the sleepiest dog in the Pacific Ocean. I'm watching Plymouth nap in the skinny shade of a portside fender. It's not the rabbit-chasing-dream kind of dog nap. I'd take him for dead if not for the gentle rise and fall of his rib cage.

Has there been a change in his behavior since the storm? Before, I didn't pay him much attention beyond the passing pat on the head. Clearly, he's upset. But is it just the weather (too hot for so much fur), or does he sense the gravity of his circumstances?

Gideon says Plymouth is part Saint Bernard. Funny, I would have guessed beagle. It's in the markings, not the size, Gideon insists. I insist that if Plymouth is a Saint Bernard, he ought to do a better job of rescuing us and bringing me tiny barrels of brandy while we wait.

In the evenings, Plymouth wakes up and sticks his head through the guardrails, barking from time to time at something below us neither Gideon or I can see. Phantom sea-mailmen? I have suspicions otherwise and it makes the hair on the back of my neck rise like the first touch from something deep-water-cold and deliberate.

From the notebook of Captain C.J. Wyle, February 14

I have come to suspect two things about Gideon. First, I suspect that Gideon is not his real name. It's a terribly inappropriate handle for someone so gawky, so freckled, so sullen. Even when he was in the womb, his parents must have known better. I broached this subject delicately this morning while we were sunning ourselves topside, or as he likes to call it, "Keeping lookout for rescue parties."

"Was Plymouth always called Plymouth?" I asked.

Upon hearing his name, the dog moved his tongue back into his heat-addled mouth and wagged his tail.

"What do you mean?" Gideon asked.

"What I said. Has this animal, now or prior, in this state or any other, been known by a different name?"

"Yeah. When I got him from the shelter he had another name," Gideon said.

"And you elected to change it on his behalf? Did you consult with him first?"

"He's my dog, I can call him what I want."

I conceded this was fair.

"Besides," Gideon said, "some names are just stupid names."

"Such as?"

Gideon tousled the dog's too-long ears.

"Andrew, for one," he said.

"That is indeed a terrible name for a dog," I agreed.

I asked him how he'd settled on the new title instead.

"It's from the Bible," Gideon said. He said it the way little boys state facts they believe ought to be obvious to everyone everywhere and how could you be so dumb?

This is the other thing I suspect of Gideon, that he is not of age. What age he isn't of, I can't be sure. Certainly not of drinking age. Voting age, maybe. That he is not yet of shaving-regularly age doesn't help his case. We've been rationing water for ten days and the best he's managed in that time is some chin scruff.

But the point I'm trying to make is that Gideon is a very private individual. Not one to talk about his personal life. Then, who is? But I have this amazing ability—a super power if you will. It turns out, when I am trapped at sea on a trimaran for two weeks with just one other person, I can see into that person's inner-most being.

What do I know about Gideon? Somewhere, a sunny antiseptic suburb is missing a punk kid. A black-jeans-wearing, Dead-Kennedys-listening, establishment-dissing, animal rights-espousing cliché with a skateboard.

Too much of a boy for the pirating life. But oh, these "oceanic activists," they'll take anyone with a student ID card, slap a life jacket on them, and call them an "intern." When I first came to this conclusion, I was horrified for Gideon, taken advantage of like that.

"Do your parents know where you are?" I asked.

"No one knows where I am!" he shouted.

From the notebook of Captain C.J. Wyle, February 15

A trimaran, in case you don't know, is a kind of sailboat with three hulls. There's one big hull in the middle where all the stuff goes—the rooms, the pipes, the wires, the food, the maps, the spoons, the salad forks, the people, etc. On either side are two smaller hulls. They are like little hull training wheels. When the boat is floating along straight up and down, they barely touch the water. Only when we tip sharply to one side or the other, does an auxiliary hull make itself useful. I keep thinking there is a metaphor to be drawn from this. But I can't decide what for.

My earlier notes indicate that this particular trimaran was a gift to SOSM from a generous leftist entrepreneur who once used it to sail around the world in some manner of record time. It should be noted that he was assisted by a crew of six for this task, none of whom were journalists, teenagers, or dogs.

To keep the craft light, and the sport of racing pure, the Artemis does not have a motor. There is an engraving at the helm to remind us this (as if we could forget). In narrow calligraphy, it says "At the mercy of the winds and our wits. Godspeed." Or, that's what it used to say. Gideon has since destroyed the offending inscription, jabbing at it one night with a Bic pen until the letters began to chip away, the pen fell apart, and his own hands could do no more good. Now it is only a jagged wooden scar, streaked with black ink and knuckle blood. Our new motto. Our epitaph.

From the notebook of Captain C.J. Wyle, February 17

My knowledge of oceanography is limited. Ditto for cartography, marine biology, maritime law, and even basic geography. Never before have I regretted my liberal arts education with such immediacy. Sailboats cannot be piloted by rigorous discourse on Kant or Wittgenstein.

Foucault would have loved this predicament, I like to think.

My fourth grade science book was called *The Oceans* and had a picture of a coral reef on the front with a single tropical fish. The fish was peeking out from behind the reef, like he'd just been caught in the act of something embarrassing. If only I could remember what was inside that tome so clearly.

What's the difference between a dolphin and a porpoise? What makes phosphorescents light up? Is a shark a mammal or a fish? The Polynesians invented the sailboat. Somewhere near here is the world's deepest ocean trench. Squid can hear through their eyes. Yes, that's right, I know about the way you watch and listen at the same time.

From the notebook of Captain C.J. Wyle, February 18

As a practical measure, Gideon and I have divided the Artemis in half. He gets the front with the crew's quarters, galley, and navigation suite. I get the back with the captain's berth, the head, and a room filled with various important-looking boat parts.

Plymouth is free to roam where he wants. Despite my threats, I wish him no harm. In fact, I like having him sleep in my cabin at night. He is pleasant company. And his breathing covers up other sounds—wave-lapping and ship-creaking and tentacle-suctioning and such.

Gideon and I are both guilty of trespassing, however. Early on after the storm, I snuck into the galley and took all of the Crystal Light lemonade packets in hopes of warding off scurvy. They are stashed beneath my (formerly C.J. Wyle's) mattress. I've also gone through most of the crew's footlockers and pilfered the items I like. Gideon appeared yesterday wearing a Panama hat I'd already taken from either Erica or Nelson, so clearly he's been in here too. But I didn't say anything about it. Thieves make terrible police.

Then, today, I caught Gideon in my own quarters. He was riffling about in the captain's shelves. I grabbed him by his studded belt and threatened him with Court Martial.

"This is high treason, sailor," I said.

He apologized and explained he was only looking for the manual.

I told him there was a manual for the espresso machine in the galley, and that I had last seen it under the cast iron skillet along with *The Joy of Cooking*.

"No," he said, "the manual for the boat."

From the notebook of Captain C.J. Wyle, February 23

This ocean reminds me of someplace I've been before. I don't want to give the impression that I am one of those worldly, traveling reporters, always on assignment to exotic locales. I've visited Hemingway's Paris, yes, and hated it. I spent one semester during college in central northern Europe for my major in western studies. I've been to Trinidad, but not Tobago. And I've only seen one species of penguin in the wild.

But somehow this spot—this water and sky and nothing else—is so familiar. I've decided it's not what's here, but what is absent that I am recalling. Although that's a depressing way to consider my life on the whole.

I hate to think I've always been this adrift.

I've just now remembered I have parents who are disappointed. I have a half-finished novel in a drawer. I have dirty dishes in a shallow apartment sink. A single neglected houseplant. A certificate that reads "One Year Sober." A nug of hash I was too anxious to take on the plane, squirreled away in the glove compartment of my car in Lot C16 at Boston Logan. Unreturned phone calls. I have loans I'll never pay back.

I'd gladly trade all my Crystal Light packets for that hash.

From the notebook of Captain C.J. Wyle, February 25

Gideon has been feeding the squid. He drops overboard my post-meal scraps of fish that even Plymouth rejects.

"I'm trying to teach the octopus to eat out of my hand," he explained when I questioned him about this behavior.

"I don't think squid eat fish," I told him. "I think they primarily eat plankton, which they suck in through their strainer-like teeth."

But my doubt did nothing to discourage the boy and after a few moments, bubbles the size of dinner plates appeared at the surface. Something had taken Gideon's offering.

From the notebook of Captain C.J. Wyle, February 26

Have you ever seen a humpback whale? They are ugly as sin. Really and truly unattractive creatures. Not that this justifies their being shot at from boats and then hacked up and refined into restorative powders and sold by the ounce to Japanese businessmen. I'm just saying this cause might be easier to get behind if the animal in question were a bit cuddlier. Or at the very least, not covered in humps.

Yet, through it all, Gideon has remained loyal, insisting that his fellow crewmates perished in the name of maritime justice.

"But what about us, then?" I ask.

Gideon is not, as a general rule, tolerant of this style of questioning.

I worry I've ceased to be an objective observer of this trip and its crew (living and not). I feel badly about this. Clearly, I am in breach of my original contract with *Popular Anarchist Quarterly*, having become too personally involved with my subject matter. Yesterday, I got out my tape recorder and tried to interview Plymouth about the mission statement of the organization and its aims for the future. He chose not to speak on the record. Pity. I have been thinking that perhaps if I can make sense of my earlier notes, I could still file my story via message-in-a-bottle. But the words on those wrinkled yellow pages appear as hieroglyphics. They are from another time and make no sense in this new, modern world. My handwriting doesn't even look like that anymore.

From the notebook of Captain C.J. Wyle, February 27

I'd like to make an amendment to my last entry, if I may. The truth of it is, even if I could file my story, I wouldn't want to. Because I didn't do what I was supposed to do. I'm here on the Artemis, yes, but that wasn't my assignment. My assignment was to follow Erica and her crew and report back on their vision, their methods, their passions, their most human moments. That's what it means to be embedded.

I should have been on the Righteous Fury when it motored bravely into that storm. I should have been at the very front, camera and tape recorder at the ready.

But instead, when Erica handed me my life jacket, I handed it right back. Not because I knew anything about the impending storm, but simply and inexcusably because I was afraid. I didn't even know what there was to be afraid of but I knew I was afraid and so I said, "No, I'll be just fine watching from the boat with Gideon, thanks." And off they went, without me, rendering my very being on the trip purposeless.

Of all the many, many things I've been ashamed of in my life, I suspect this is perhaps the most shameful of all. The reason: no one knows I've done it but me and I still feel ashamed.

From the notebook of Captain C.J. Wyle, March 2

Water has become a problem. The greatest irony of the ocean is… do I even need to say it? Every morning, we ration out our daily liquids into shot glasses. I've given up on the trick of swallowing my own spit for sustenance; the placebo of it's gone and I'm only left thirstier.

Gideon's been thinking about trying to drink his own piss a la Kevin Costner in *Waterworld*. I see him eyeing the near-amber stream he allows to trickle off the side of the boat every fourteen hours or so. But Mr. Costner had a special machine for that, I remind him. He reminds me not to watch while he pees.

From the notebook of Captain C.J. Wyle, March 3

I wonder about the individuals with whom we used to share this boat. What kind of people choose the seafaring life, anyway? They say the ocean is the last refuge of the damned.

No, that's prayer. Prayer is the last refuge of the damned. Regardless.

Sometimes, Gideon stands on the deck with his head back, arms spread, baggy t-shirt hanging from his sun-blistered shoulders like a sail. What is he offering up?

Or beckoning in?

I don't want to be alone out here either.

From the notebook of Captain C.J. Wyle, March 4

Gideon has begun jettisoning things into the sea. First, his video camera, battery-power long since exhausted. Then pots and pans, socks and shoes, etc. He thinks if the boat is lighter, it will have an easier time floating somewhere, as if it were the weight that holds us to the middle of the ocean.

"That looks fun," I told him after he tossed a half-gallon jug of hand sanitizer over the side of the boat this morning. He didn't answer me, but I decided to join in anyway.

Inside the cabin—which had already grown muggy and airless in the heat—I moved aside boxes of charts and nautical instruments until I found the corpse of the Artemis' shipboard communication system.

Early on in the trip, Erica dismantled the radio, saying any attempt to contact authorities for any purpose would be considered an act of mutiny. At the time, this proclamation seemed foolhardy, but as an observer and not an active crewmember, I didn't feel it was my place to object. Now I'm pretty pissed about it though.

I pushed the stray knobs and fuses back into their metal casing, picked the whole contraption up, then tied its chords into a ball and carried it back up top. It wasn't a particularly heavy device, but it made a cathartic splash none the less.

"Hey! Hey, what the fuck?" Gideon barked. "I was using that."

I kicked over the few extra pieces that had fallen to the deck, tidying up.

"What the fuck?" Gideon said again. "What's wrong with you?"

"Sorry, pal. Didn't know you were playing dollhouse with it. I promise I'll get you some new Lincoln Logs for Christmas."

"I wasn't playing. I was fixing it. I was going to fix it." His skinny hands balled tight into skinny fists, cracked fingernails digging into his own flesh. He looked as if he might hit me.

"I ought to throw *you* overboard," he said. He unclenched his hands and took hold of the hem of my shirt. His grip was surprisingly light. I made no move to shake him off.

"You weren't going to fix the radio," I said. "It was a useless, broken thing."

"You're a useless, broken thing!" Gideon's voice split on "broken." His breath smelled like an old man's, like something was decaying inside of him. I noticed for the first time that Gideon has lost two teeth since the start of the trip—fairly prominent ones. Blood leaked from his gums as he spoke. I felt around in my own mouth with my tongue to see if I had suffered a similar misfortune, but everything seemed intact.

"Nope, still okay," I said.

Gideon blinked twice, shaking his head. He let go of my shirt and turned away from me, stomping across the deck to where Plymouth lay dozing, unaware of what had just transpired. I watched Gideon nuzzle his face against the dog and whisper conspiratorially to him. After a moment, Plymouth responded with a volley of face licks.

From the notebook of Captain C.J. Wyle, March 5

Today, Gideon is giving me the silent treatment. He refuses to leave his quarters except to cook and eat. I worry he may be ill. The quiet is eerie and I find myself willing Plymouth to bark just for distraction.

Shortly after dusk, I opened Gideon's door and asked if he wanted to play cards, maybe some Old Maid or Go Fish. He only glared at me from his narrow cot, burrowing his body deeper into the stale sheets.

I've concluded the youth today have no patience for games of chance.

From the notebook of Captain C.J. Wyle, March 6

Last night, the wind picked up again and I could hear the sky eating up the stars, cannibalizing itself. From my bed, I yelled to Gideon to raise the sails, thinking we might use those early gusts to push us somewhere. He yelled back that I ought to go fuck myself.

For hours, we bobbed back and forth. I am getting pretty good at not puking in such conditions. I lay in bed, thinking still and level thoughts, and listening to the Artemis creak and shudder. At the worst of it, I was convinced I heard the suction cups. It's come to pull us apart as an ally of the ocean, I thought. But there was no added violence from the squid. It was as if he'd found us, lonely in the storm, and was just holding on.

From the notebook of Captain C.J. Wyle, March 7

This morning, Gideon came down into my berth, dragging behind him all the line from the main sail.

"I'm going to lasso the octopus," he announced. It was the second time he'd spoken to me in three days.

"Excellent," I said. "That will be good eating."

"No. I am going to lasso it so it will pull us with it to shore."

I told him squid don't live on shore. They live on the bottom of the ocean. This much I am sure of. I remember the page from my science book—colorful, with drawings and a fact box in bold text asking, "Did you know?" This knowledge is unsoiled by childhood forgetfulness or adult self-doubt. "I stake my reputation on it," I said.

Gideon shook his head. No, he insisted, if only he could get a line around the octopus, it would take us someplace safe.

I looked into his jaundiced eyes. Crusted and earnest, they begged for something far, far beyond my capacity to deliver. Why hadn't he ever asked before? I reached out and let my hand rest at the base of Gideon's neck. I patted him between his jutting shoulder blades. People who are friends do this for one another. I've seen video footage of it. I remember a different place where I knew what it felt like to be touched and held.

I told Gideon I would help. I told him it was the best plan anyone had come up with.

We tied a giant slipknot and anchored the rope to the guardrails (all the cleats are gone, if you recall). I shook Plymouth awake and clicked and whistled for him to join us. It seemed important that everyone be present. Gideon dropped our best rations overboard, wiping fish remnants and coffee grounds off his hands onto his shirt and then removing the neon garment and placing it into the sea as well.

We sat together at the bow of the Artemis, in the aching sunlight, waiting.

SPUD

SPUD II

May 21, 2077, Outer Space
Lieutenant Colonel Parker Timothy Olstead

He thinks this is what it might feel like to be out at sea. Vast. Surrounded by mysteries both above and below. Lonesome, but in a pleasant way—the kind of way that makes you a better man.

This is also how he likes to describe his job, when he gives talks and lectures for students, aspiring scientists and astronauts alike: *We're the new Magellans*, he says. *We explore uncharted places. We go to the limits of the known world, then we go further.* By limits, he means both physical distance, but also intellectual distance, and personal, psychological distance. Going to space is hard. It tests you in degrees you wouldn't expect. Sometimes he explains this concept; sometimes he leaves it unsaid, hoping his young audiences can make the leap themselves.

And here he is again, pressing those very limits. Particularly the personal ones.

He'd launched with two Swedes and a dozen cephalopods from the base at Vidsel the morning before. He spent the days prior working with his soon-to-be shuttlemates, Annika and Edvard, as they prepared for their departure. One evening, in the name of collegial small talk, they told him their favorite part of any shuttle mission was the launch itself.

"There's this humming that happens within you," Edvard said. "Like the sound of each one of your cells vibrating. When else will you ever have the chance to experience that? Never."

"A launch is truly a thing to be savored and enjoyed," Annika added.

But he disagreed. He likes the part immediately after the launch better— the first twenty-four hours up in zero gravity. Because it feels like being on a boat in the middle of the ocean. Obviously, their shuttle, the Krona Ark III, has complex navigation systems, keeping them in constant communication with a team back on Earth who monitor all aspects of their health and travel. But still, the feeling is the same: that, in their isolation, they really are totally adrift. They have to orient themselves to their new surroundings and rely on their wits and on each other to succeed. And there's something both powerful and humbling in that feeling.

When he explained this, the Swedes had nodded in a way he hoped meant they thought this sentiment wise. But it also could have meant they were just humoring him. He hasn't quite figured them out yet. And so, he's kept a professional distance, both during their time at the base in northern Sweden, and now aboard the shuttle, a full day into their mission. He is pleasant but detached. He doesn't get too personal.

But if he were inclined to get personal, there are two things, at the forefront of his mind, he might tell them.

The first thing is that he's never actually been to sea.

Sure, he's been on boats, but only in Washington's Puget Sound. So, here he is, a marine biologist by training and a man who frequently compares himself to the oceanic explorers of yore, who has never actually been in the heart of an ocean. It is a source of great shame to him and something he would like to confide in someone about, if only he felt comfortable enough with anyone to confide such a thing to them. He has never met such a person.

The second thing is his son, who he does not yet know, but who occupies all his thoughts, distracts him from the work he is really here to do.

His son is the reason he tries now to think of the sea. This is the part of the shuttle mission where he should be feeling most at sea. Really getting into it. Digging the sensation. He does his best to focus on this idea, to coax his excitement back. But no such luck. He floats around the cabin, listless, hoping his fellow astronauts will not notice his malaise.

When the shuttle mission was initially offered to him, he'd been thrilled, and also flattered. He knows to be a part of the first collaboration between NASA and the budding Swedish space program is an honor. Though NASA has always employed marine biologists, it's only in the last decade they've begun to see the value in sending them into space. He's one of the first to really make his mark in the field. Still, he was surprised the Swedes had picked him, of all possible American scientists, to join the team on the Krona Ark III and pursue any line of research he wished with the support of the Swedish crew. He has chosen to investigate how the bacteria that live on the flesh of squid react to a zero-gravity environment. He's selected twelve different species, including his personal favorite, the rare Nordic squid, to be transported in cylindrical tanks of varying size with self-sealing lids. The tanks are here with him now, locked into place on his workstation in the shuttle's main cabin. The squid appear docile and content.

If only he could direct his attention to his colleagues aboard the Krona Ark III, or the plethora of creatures he's brought for study. Instead, his mind and heart are three hundred miles below in a laboratory at the University of Michigan where genetic data from his own blood is replicating itself at a biologically predetermined pace. *His son*, as both he and the UM doctors refer to the project. But really, so much more than a son. So much closer. Although the boy, along with his peers, will live and go to school at the lab, the program director has assured him that donor parents such as himself—all scientists, artists, thinkers of note—will be allowed to visit whenever they want. Of course, right now, the child is nothing but a fetus floating in a transparent vat of gelatinous material designed to simulate the experience of a real human womb. He has been to visit numerous times and has trouble seeing a resemblance between himself and the particular fetus they say is his. Still, he imagines reading to the boy from picture books, teaching him to play catch, taking him on visits to the aquarium. Maybe, someday, they could even learn to sail together. Get out into the real ocean together.

He imagines the day, slated for six weeks from now, when the lab director will pull the baby from its womb vat, wrap it in a blue blanket, and hand it to him. He imagines holding the baby to his chest, feeling his warm little body against him. He wants that day to be today. At the very least, he would like to be back in the lab in the company of the fetus in the vat. He does not like being apart from him in this way—literally the farthest he could possibly be. Fatherly protectiveness, he thinks.

He knows he should focus on the task at hand. There will be plenty of time to think about the boy later, once he's back on terra firma. Now though, he has much to learn from his squid. He convinces himself it is time to stop all this sad floating around and get to work. He straps himself into the chair at his workstation and is about to pick one of the squid from his collection for analysis when Annika and Edvard enter the main cabin, looking grim.

"We think there is a small problem," Annika says.

Then the lights go out, the command console goes blank, and the hum of the shuttle's life support system ceases. The endless foreign chatter from Visdel is silenced. Everything is very quiet.

Now it really is like we're at sea, he thinks. They are cut adrift. They will have to rely on their wits. They will have to navigate by the stars. And when they return home, it will be with tales of great heroism to tell their loved ones—like cresting a rogue wave, or vanquishing a giant serpent. It will make a good story for the boy, when he's old enough to hear it.

He doesn't say this to his crewmates, of course. But it's a thought he takes pleasure in, and he squirrels it away for later. Something to come back to again once true fear takes hold.

Tiger, Tiger

Something is amiss at the Rolson Meth Lab.

Though, to be fair, something is always amiss over there. That's why we call it the Meth Lab, as opposed to the Rolson estate or the Rolson's place or the That Lovely Home Where the Delightful Mr. Rolson Lives.

My wife and I can't agree on what's making the sound, or even what type of sound it is. I say it's mechanical—the cold rumble of an ancient tractor engine starting then dying, starting then dying, over and over. This would make sense. Chet Rolson, the Meth Lab's proprietor, is a collector of well-used farm equipment. Ditto for junked cars. I see him tinkering with them in his front yard from time to time.

But Jenny insists the sound is the cry of something living. It's a distressed mammal. It's hungry. It's angry. She holds to this belief and the sounds have become very upsetting to her.

"They're torturing that poor thing," she says.

"What poor thing?"

"That poor thing. Whatever it is, they're torturing it."

"Maybe that's the sound it's supposed to make. Maybe it's a perfectly healthy and happy thing. Whatever it is," I say.

She shakes her head. "Nothing that makes a sound like that could be happy. Just listen to it. I'm an animal. You're an animal. Animals know when other animals are in trouble. It's instinct."

"But it's not an animal," I tell her. "It's a threshing machine. Granted, they may very well be torturing that threshing machine."

Jenny does not appreciate my attempt at levity.

"I'm not kidding, Mark," she says. Her facial expression confirms this.

Jenny is one of those women whose sympathy for living things is unconditional. Any time a dog or cat is discovered lost in the neighborhood, she champions the effort for its safe return, printing fliers and insisting we house it until the owners can be contacted. We've acquired two cats this way, Boomer and Travis. Once, Jenny found an injured fox pup in the front yard. She built it a nest in a cardboard box and nursed it back to health.

"You're such a caring soul," I tell her.

"It's my maternal instinct," she says, looking everywhere except at me.

"Would you like me to go over to Rolson's and ask what's going on? Because I will, if it will make you feel better," I tell her.

She says no, and I am relieved.

The Rolson Meth Lab is a dilapidated white farmhouse. The paint is peeling and the front porch is bowed. It is, even for a passerby, a place of unsettling noises and smells, some human, some not. Chet Rolson is the only full-time resident. Sometimes there's a woman around: Chet's girlfriend. Shortly after we moved in, the couple had a series of loud and upsetting fights that once ended with police intervention, but no charges pressed. Things have been quiet between them lately though. There's a pair of shifty looking dudes who hang around on the front steps most days, others who come and go, and, from time to time, a middle school-aged boy with a BMX bike. We believe this is Chet's son. That Chet Rolson could have partial custody of a kid is horrifying to me. Doubly so to Jenny, who has suggested we call Child Protective Services, but worries we won't be able to provide sufficiently damning evidence to warrant investigation. All we have is speculation and conjecture. What actually goes on at Chet Rolson's house is a mystery to us.

Needless to say, we're pretty sure he's making meth in there.

I don't want to give the impression we live in a dodgy part of town. I've been in Indiana for seven years and it seems to me our rural suburb is pretty much the same as every other suburb in this predominantly rural state. I imagine an aerial view must look like someone puked up Monopoly pieces in a field. There's no real sense of planning or consistency. Clapboard houses sit at varying distances from Derring Street, our main thoroughfare. Behind the homes on our side of the street runs a sprawling corporate soybean farm. Our immediate neighbors to the right, the Wengers, keep chickens. In our own backyard, Jenny has cultivated a truly excellent garden. Jenny and I moved here from Bloomington shortly after we got married. We bought the biggest house we could afford with the intention of "growing into it." Three years later, it's still just the two of us, plus the cats.

The Rolson Meth Lab aside, our neighbors are a quiet and drama-free crowd. They're almost all large families, with the exception of the Wengers who are, like Jenny and me, a childless couple. But being well into their sixties, people have probably stopped asking them all the fucking time when they plan to reproduce.

Tom and Darcy Wenger invite Jenny and me over for Sunday lunch every week after church even though we don't go to church. "Come by after church and we'll put together a little spread," Darcy says each Sunday morning, appearing on our porch, presumably on her way to the local house of the Lord. "Okay," we say, "will do." Lunch is always lovely and our absence at church is never discussed. It has recently occurred to me that maybe the Wengers don't go either.

The Rolson Meth Lab is a hot topic with the Wengers. Chet Rolson's property borders theirs on the other side and they are privy to all sorts of oddity that stays under the radar for the rest of Derring Street.

"I'm sure you've been hearing all that howling going on," Darcy says almost as soon as we sit down to eat. "It must be keeping the whole block up half the night."

Her use of the word "howling" signals to me that she, too, has pegged the sound as animal. This conversation will follow Jenny and me home, I'm certain. I want to change the subject, but I know it won't do any good. Darcy always finds a path back to talking about whatever she wants to talk about.

"That man, I swear, it's always something," Darcy says.

Jenny stops eating her egg salad sandwich and leans forward. "Do you know what it is? What's making the sound?" she asks.

"No," says Darcy, "but there's a cage."

Jenny puts her hand to her mouth.

"I'm positive he's got a creature locked up back there," Darcy continues, though I wish she wouldn't. "Me personally, I think it sounds like a lion."

"It's not a lion," Tom says.

"Tom's been on safari and he says that's not what a lion sounds like," Darcy says, "but I got a glimpse of it over the fence the other day. I think a lion probably has different cries in captivity than it does out in the wild. Don't you think, Tom?"

"It's not a lion," Tom replies with his usual curtness. The man is the picture-perfect Middle American husband. Hard working, silent, long-faced, he may well have been the model for "American Gothic," if the picture featured a curly-haired gossip for the farmer's bride.

"Can we have a look at the cage?" Jenny asks.

"Of course, hon," Darcy says, as sweet as if Jenny had just requested seconds on pie.

Single-file, the four of us walk out the Wengers' back door to the tall picket fence that divides the two properties. We line up, faces pressed to the fence's slats. I imagine Darcy doing this every afternoon, making *tsk*ing sounds and taking mental notes on the Rolson crew's comings and goings to share with the rest of the neighborhood.

There's a shed and some patchy grass dotted with a few pieces of rusted farming tools.

"Look, Jenny," I say. "I think that thing on the far left is a threshing machine."

She hisses at me to be quiet even though there's no one around except the Wengers to hear me.

"See back by the trees?" Darcy says. "That's where the cage is."

Sure enough, tucked between a cluster of maple trees and half covered with a blue tarp is a big damn cage, all metal with wrist-thick bars. It looks like the kind circus animals get carted around in, like the cartoons on Animal Crackers boxes. From our vantage point at the fence, the interior of the cage is dark and still. It could hold a large, violent, angry animal. It also could be empty.

"How long has the cage been there?" I ask. "Has it maybe just always been there?"

"Oh Lord, I have absolutely no idea," Darcy admits.

At home, Jenny is distressed.

"What if it escapes?" she wants to know.

"What if what escapes from where?"

"Mark, we're not playing this game anymore," she says.

I remind her we don't know for certain that there's anything in the cage.

"Who keeps a cage without an animal inside?"

"Who keeps cars without wheels and tractors that don't run? Same guy."

"It's not safe," she says. "It's not safe and it's not humane and it's not right."

I have no answer to this.

"We should call animal control," she says.

"And tell them what? The weirdo down the road has a circus cage in his yard and something that may or may not be inside the cage is making strange sounds? We don't call CPS about the boy, but we're going to call Animal Control about an unidentified noise?"

"You don't have to get snippy," Jenny says.

"I'm not getting snippy," I say, fully aware of how snippy this sounds. "I'm just trying to make a point."

"And what point is that? Doing nothing is better than something?"

"In some cases, yeah," I say. "Sometimes it's safer just to wait and see."

"I'm not entirely sure what we're waiting for," she says. But she doesn't move to get the phone or look up a number. So, conversation over.

On Monday, Jenny leaves for work at seven in the morning, like always. I sleep another four hours before I get up to start my own "work." I use the term loosely here. In our home office, I am supposedly occupied with finishing my book. I quit my job as the assistant editor of our local weekly newspaper six months ago, with Jenny's blessing, expressly for this purpose. We have a little savings and Jenny's salary is enough to support us for now. The time off and the completion of a long project would do me good, Jenny insisted. Initially, I agreed. Mostly though, I spend my days drinking coffee, petting the cats, reading the *New York Times* online, and watching YouTube videos. There's a lot of guilt. I'm not sure what good this is doing anyone.

I'm playing Get-the-String with Boomer and Travis when the doorbell rings Friday afternoon. It's Tom Wenger. I open the door, smiling my most neighborly smile, expecting him to say the wife sent him over to see if we'd like some lemon cake as she'd made too much. Or something of that nature.

"It's a tiger," Tom says.

I want to be surprised by this announcement. I want to act like I don't know what he means, appearing on my doorstep and talking about tigers here in the middle of Indiana on such a lovely spring day.

"Okay," I say. "Let's go have a look."

In the Wengers' yard, Tom and I join Darcy at the fence and peer into Rolson's property.

"Do you see it?" Darcy asks, her voice wobbly with excitement.

"No," I say. The cage is dim and still, just as it was at Sunday lunch.

"Come stand where I am," Darcy says.

We switch places, but I can't see any further into the enclosure. I'm about to call both Wengers out as agitators and liars when I catch a glimpse of something in the murky darkness. I can't see all of it at once, just a wisp of orange-brown fur, maybe an eye, maybe a paw. Maybe a jagged black stripe. Then it's gone, back into the recesses of its horrible home.

"Holy fucking fuck," I say.

I ask the Wengers what they plan to do, what action will be taken. Neither moves their face from the fence to answer.

Back at the house, I am restless. Writing is out of the question. I feed the cats, water the plants, and take out the trash. I watch the clock and think about what it will be like when Jenny comes home and I have to tell her what I saw. Contrary to my wishes, this thing isn't going away. It's only getting larger, taking shape—a tiger shape. It occurs to me that a different sort of man might simply keep this new information to himself and spare his sensitive wife the agony of knowing exactly what it is that haunts her. Unfortunately, I am not that man. Jenny and I tell each other almost everything.

But I figure I can at least put the conversation off for a while.

I call Derek, a friend from journalism school who works in Bloomington, to see if he wants to meet up somewhere for drinks after he gets off work. I tell him I'm more than happy to come in to the city. He reminds me that another former classmate, Ethan, recently moved nearby—less than ten miles from me and Jenny, in fact. I feel guilty for having forgotten, for not having sought him out sooner.

The three of us make plans to meet. I send Jenny a text message: "Going out with the guys, be home late." Though this must come as a surprise to her, she replies, "Okay! Have fun!"

And in spite of myself, I do. We talk about movies we've seen and IU's basketball prospects. We reminisce just enough about the people we went to school with, the late nights we spent in the university's dreary basement news lab, and the Cinco de Mayo party where Jenny and I first met. Derek tells the story of a colleague of his who got caught with a cache of porn on his office computer and Ethan gives me a list of albums he thinks I might enjoy. No one mentions big cats, or any other kind of wild animal for that matter.

At one point, Derek does say, "I was sorry to hear about the baby and everything." I thank him for his concern and realize just how long it's been since I've seen these guys. At least a year.

When I come in, Jenny is already asleep, curled on her side with my pillow clutched between her arms. She is by nature a cuddler, a seeker of warm spaces. I take off my clothes and slide under the blankets beside her, gently wresting the pillow from her grasp. She reaches an arm around my chest to take its place.

"I'm glad you're home," she murmurs, kissing my neck.

This is the way it would be with our children, too, were we to have any. Jenny would hold them close. A safe corner of the world for her family, a brood of loved ones to draw near—these are Jenny's highest aspirations. And I keep her from them.

Jenny wants a kid. Jenny wants multiple kids. Jenny wants a minivan full of kids. And I thought I did, too, until Jenny got pregnant. Or rather, until Jenny stopped being pregnant. We say miscarriage, but by seven months along that's not really what it is. At seven months, it's a death. It's the loss of someone we'd given a name and begun assigning attributes to. We'd say things like, "I hope she gets my eyes and your pleasant disposition," or whathaveyou.

This was hard for both of us. But Jenny is an optimistic person. A stick-with-it person. A when-the-going-gets-tough-the-tough-get-going person. I admire this about my wife. I am certain these are the qualities that would make her a good parent. These are not qualities I see in myself. This knowledge has made me reconsider our plans.

Jenny thinks I, like her, am still grieving, and when I'm done grieving, we'll pick up with the baby-making where we left off. She's right about the grief part.

For breakfast, Jenny makes buttermilk pancakes and asks how things are with Derek and Ethan. I give her the updates plus the latest gossip on others from the old group. Callen is teaching English in South Korea, Sophie is trying to sell a screenplay, Jack is engaged to a woman no one likes, and that thing in the cage is a tiger.

"A tiger?"

"It looks that way," I say. I tell her about the day before with Tom and Darcy.

"So you saw it, then?" she asks. "You actually *saw* a living, breathing tiger?"

"I saw something," I say. Suddenly though, I am not sure just what exactly it is that I saw. In my mind's eye, the tiger-like form shifts. It's a mangy dog. It's a pile of gunnysacks. It's an inflatable pool toy. I find it impossible to speak with clarity on the subject. This comes as a relief. I am an unreliable witness, unfit for further questioning.

"I can't be certain though," I say.

"You said a tiger."

"Tom said a tiger. I think I was influenced by his power of suggestion. You know, like, the idea of a tiger was in my head so I saw one."

"And now you're not so sure."

"Exactly."

"But you did see *something*?"

"Yes," I agree. I did see something.

"Mark, this is ridiculous," she says. "Tiger or no tiger, we have a right to feel safe in our own neighborhood, in our own home."

Again, I offer to just go over and ask Chet about his alleged tiger if it will make her feel better. This time she doesn't say no. This time she says, "Yes, it would make me feel better."

We are slow to finish breakfast. Once the dishes are done, we drive into town together to return library books and browse at the nursery. Back home, I help Jenny in the garden. I change a dead light bulb in the basement and mow the front lawn.

After every activity, I ask myself, "Is this the appropriate moment to go confront our likely drugged-out and potentially hostile neighbor about the creature he may or may not be harboring in his backyard?"

Each time the answer comes back "no." So I don't. I lie on the couch with Jenny and the cats, reading and doing crossword puzzles. We cook another meal and eat on the porch so we can watch the sunset. As I clear the dishes, a howl snakes through the neighborhood, feral and mean. I expect Jenny to say something, but she doesn't.

All the next day, I don't go talk to Chet. Nor do I talk to him the day after that. But then on Tuesday, fate, or just stupid coincidence, puts Chet and me in the same place at the same time and I've got no excuse not to say something.

With Jenny at work during the weekdays, I am the default runner of errands, doer of chores. I don't mind. It gives me something to occupy the time I should spend writing. It's at the grocery store that I find Chet.

As soon as I get out of my car, I see him skulking across the parking lot, two bulging plastic bags in each hand and the boy five paces behind him, his double in miniature. For a second, I consider getting back in the car and driving away before he sees me. But then I remember that Chet isn't looking for me, couldn't give a fuck if I'm in the parking lot or not. It's me who's looking for him.

I wait until they've reached their truck before I approach. He's loading his groceries into the cab, his son already installed in the passenger seat.

"Hey, Chet," I say, nice and casual, like maybe I'm just passing by on my way into the store, which I am.

He turns and gives me a neighborly head nod. We are neighbors after all, even if we never speak and my wife and I sometimes spy on him through the slats of his fence after Sunday lunch.

"Hey, Chet," I say again, but with a different inflection. More purposeful.

He stops. He turns his whole body around and looks a lot less neighborly.

"Yeah?" he says.

"Quick question, Chet."

"Yeah?"

I don't know how to proceed. The boy, perhaps sensing something in his father's tone he wants no part of, slips out the passenger side door and walks past us.

"Jake," Chet calls to him. "Don't go far. We're leaving."

The boy nods.

Chet turns to me again. "Yeah?" he asks once more.

"Are you keeping a wild animal on your property?"

Chet looks at me for a long time, his eyes squinty under the brim of his ball cap. "Come again?" he asks. Then he spits. He literally spits. The loogie lands not on my feet, but very near to them as if we were characters in an old Western movie, squaring off for a showdown.

"Look man, someone's going to call the cops. I'm surprised they haven't already," I say, although this is actually a lie. I am not surprised at all.

"I've got a permit for it," Chet says.

"You can't get a permit for something like that. It's not like a grain elevator. It's a living creature."

"Man, you don't even know what you don't know," Chet says. "You can get a permit for a fucking Burmese python in this state if you want. Orangutans, crocodiles, whatever."

"Is it a tiger?" I ask.

Chet shakes his head like he can't even believe I'm wasting his time with this line of questioning.

"It's been a pleasure talking to you, neighbor," Chet says. Then he calls to his son who has wandered back toward the store entrance to fiddle with the vending machines.

Standing next to Chet in the parking lot, I am struck by how similar we must appear to anyone passing by. We are around the same age, gaunt and lanky. Three days stubble, Carharts and boots. Unemployed and roaming the streets of town mid-afternoon on a Tuesday. Chet, with his son in tow, at least has the marker of adulthood: of having sired and raised a child. The boy is proof of some minimal success on the man's part.

At night, in bed, I raise the question with Jenny.

"Do you think Chet Rolson is more of a man than me?" I ask.

"Why? Because he owns a tiger?"

"An alleged tiger," I say.

"Regardless. I don't consider animal cruelty a sign of masculinity, no."

"But what if you just saw him walking on the street and you didn't even know about the tiger or whatever? What would you think of him?"

"What's this about?" she asks, always able to see right to the very center of me.

"Chet's boy looks an awful lot like him," I say.

"Mark, I told you I'm ready to try again whenever you are. Is this you saying you're ready?"

I lie back and look up at the ceiling. Down the road the alleged tiger screams and everything seems so fragile I expect the sound to shatter our windows, crack our wine glasses, and break our wedding china.

"No," I say. "I guess not."

Under the blankets, Jenny wraps herself around me.

"Okay," she says. "That's okay, Mark."

We fall asleep curled together like kittens.

Three days later, the cries stop entirely. A nervous quiet enshrouds the neighborhood. Or maybe it's just the same old quiet as before and I'm the one who's nervous.

Jenny is nervous, too. Have they killed it? Have they injured it so badly it is incapable of making noise? Have they allowed it to escape? Each of these prospects seems equally horrifying.

I tell her I read about a big cat sanctuary outside of Terre Haute. They have all sorts of lions, tigers, cougars, and jaguars that were once pets, but were turned over when their original owners realized they were in over their heads. Maybe Rolson took the tiger there and now it's living happily and well fed in the company of its brethren. Jenny says she'd like very much to believe that. But when we share this theory with the Wengers, Darcy insists that in her near-constant vigilance of the Rolson Meth Lab, no one has come to the house with a large van or truck or anything that might be used to transport a tiger. The cage is still in its original place, half covered by the tarp, its door shut and latched.

We check the paper each morning—the crime blotter, the local news, and a section called "Weird and Wild"—for reports of a tiger sighting, or better yet, capture by local authorities. Nothing.

"It's almost like it was never even there to begin with," I say to Jenny.

"No, it's not," she corrects me. "It's not like that at all. I can't shake it so easily."

"Me neither," I confess. "I guess I just wish that's how I felt."

"Are we still talking about the tiger here?" she asks.

I shrug. Jenny reaches across the breakfast table and puts her hand on mine. We have been so gentle with each other for so long—light touches, soft words. Even when we argue, it's in whispers. So it's a relief when, instead of letting go of my hand, Jenny squeezes hard. She pulls me out of my chair and into the bedroom, onto the bed. We push and tug at each other in the slatted morning light behind our half-drawn shades. This doesn't last long. Jenny comes with an almost primal growl I want to mimic, but I get distracted by my own orgasm and double over, my face to her chest, in silence.

That morning, for the first time in a long time, I write. My book, as I envision it, will be collection of essays about the six months I spent in Belize and southern Mexico between college and grad school. This was before I met Jenny. My girlfriend at the time had a little money and we lived in a hut on a beach, and then in a different hut on a different beach. It was her idea and then, just like now, I was supposed to be writing. The whole trip, a once-in-a-lifetime chance for me to write. It wasn't as romantic as it sounds (petty arguments, Montezuma's revenge, my passport stolen) and the desire to be honest pitted against the desire not to look like a tool who squandered six months in paradise has made my progress choppy at best.

Today, I am honest. And it's good. I write about the day my girlfriend begged me to go cliff jumping. She knew a place where the locals did it. By sunset, we'd jump off a waterfall, together, and it would reinvigorate us, she said. I was hesitant, which is a nice way of saying I was afraid. On the way, we drank American beer in the back of a pick-up truck, me feeling queasy the whole time. In the end, my girlfriend jumped off the waterfall by herself while I stood at the bottom, holding our empty bottles, worrying about what I'd say to her parents if she drowned. It's not my proudest moment, but it feels like progress to write it down. Maybe the most progress I've made in the last year.

I am thinking about my next essay when Jenny comes into the office, tears forming at the corners of her eyes.

"Mark, I can't find Boomer," she says. "I think he must have gotten out."

"Okay," I say, rising slowly from my chair like I don't think there's any cause in the world for concern about a missing cat. "Let's go have a look."

Together, we visit each of Boomer's favorite spots in the house, even though I'm certain Jenny has done this at least twice by herself already. He's not in his cat bed. He's not in the bedroom closet. He's not pressed up against the sliding glass door where the sunlight gathers this time of the day. Behind the couch, there is a visible cluster of fur, but no Boomer.

"We never vacuum back here," I say.

"When do we ever look behind the couch except when we're looking for a cat?" Jenny asks.

Travis follows us from room to room, meowing. He'd do this no matter what we were searching for, but in the absence of one cat, the presence of the other seems somehow significant. Like he knows something about it.

"I think you're right," I say to Jenny. "I think he got out."

In the yard, we call Boomer's name and rustle the low bushes that fringe our property. Jenny is crying a little again.

"Don't think like that," I say. "Hey, Jenny, he's around somewhere, okay?"

Jenny shakes her head. "He doesn't even have his claws anymore to protect himself."

There are many things that might happen to a cat in this neighborhood. Animal control could have picked him up. He could have wandered out to the highway and been hit by a car. The Rolson boy could be torturing him in the basement of his father's house while daddy cooks up a batch of drugs in the bathtub. Fuck, we really should have called someone a long time ago.

"He probably just got himself stuck under the Johnsons' porch," I say.

I point to the long driveway directly across the street from ours. It belongs to another set of neighbors we nod politely to in passing and make small talk with only if absolutely unavoidable. We walk in the direction I've just pointed.

"I don't think I'll ever feel like it's safe for the cats to be outside again," Jenny says.

"It's a good thing we don't have little kids running around to worry about," I say, and then immediately wish I could take it back. I look into my wife's eyes. I can see her anxiety turn to anger, her anger to pity, her pity to resignation, and her resignation to regret, all right in front of me in the middle of Derring Street while I call for our stupid cat.

"Shit," I say. "That's not what I mean."

"No, Mark. That is what you mean. That is exactly what you god-damn mean."

She is one hundred percent correct and I'm at a loss for how to respond.

"I'm going to check the house one more time," Jenny says, coolly, turning her back to me and walking across the street. I watch her skinny shoulders, the sun-kissed pink of her neck peeking out from behind her ponytail. I should go after her, hug her from behind and apologize not just for being insensitive, but for not being able to give her what she wants, for not being as strong as she is.

Instead I walk up to the Johnson family's house and knock on the door. No one is home so I duck down and look under their front porch, calling Boomer's name and whistling even though neither of the cats respond when I do this at home.

There is nothing beneath the porch except a coiled garden hose. I stand and cross the Johnsons' yard. At their property line, I whistle for the cat again. The family next door to the Johnsons are Jehovah's Witnesses. They keep their three children from school, educating them at home instead. I don't know if these two facts are related. When I knock on the door, it's one of the kids who answers. I feel like a child myself, explaining to an adolescent girl that I've lost my cat.

"He's gray except he's got white markings on his face and his tummy," I say. "Have you seen him at all?"

The girl shakes her head and offers a small, "I'm sorry." I wonder what she thinks of the things that happen outside her window as she's trying to study each day. The comings and goings of secular life, the Rolson boy, just about her age, tearing around on his bike.

Back on our own side of the street, Darcy Wenger says she hasn't seen Boomer either.

"You don't think maybe…"

"I'm sure he just wandered away," I say, cutting her off.

After that, I don't even consider whether to go to the next house down or not. I just do. I am not really myself in this moment. Or, rather, I am some approximation of myself. I am the diligent husband helping his wife find her beloved cat. I am knocking on my neighbors' doors, none of whom I seek to avoid, because I am a grown man and why should I be afraid of the people with whom I share a street? This is the man who walks to Chet Rolson's door and rings the bell and waits.

This is the man who, when there is no answer, knocks hard. Who calls, "Anyone home?" in a friendly yet assertive voice. Who kicks three times at the base of the door to be certain he's heard.

When still there is no answer, it is someone else entirely who twists the knob and pushes the door open.

Inside the Rolson Meth Lab, the front door opens to a shallow entryway and then the living room where Rolson's got reddish shag carpet and three couches that don't match. There's a TV, a flimsy coffee table and a bookshelf filled with a variety of items that aren't books. Plastic bags, matchbox cars, a socket wrench, an empty pastry box.

There are people in the room, too. A man and a woman I've never seen before lie head to toe on one of the couches, their arms wrapped around one another's legs, their eyes closed. Chet sits in the middle of the floor, cross-legged, his head down, chin to his chest.

Whatever they're on, it isn't meth. Or, if it is meth, then they're clearly on the come-down. Or the come-up. I actually don't know much about meth.

I stand in the doorway, just staring like an idiot until Chet notices me.

"What do you want?" he asks.

"I want to know what happened to the tiger," I say.

"What tiger?"

"The tiger you were keeping in a cage in your backyard for which you insisted you had a permit. The tiger which is now gone." I'm aware that there's a danger in getting snippy with drug users. I'm also aware that I sound like a dick. But I can't help myself. As it turns out, the version of me who has entered Rolson's house has just as little control over himself and the things he says as every other version of me.

"Well, sounds like you just answered your own question," Chet says.

"What?"

Chet picks at a scab on his lower lip and doesn't say anything else. Gone. He means the tiger is gone.

"But where did it go, Chet?" I ask.

Chet holds my gaze, but it's clear he's not actually looking at me. He's looking through me, or maybe just at the middle distance between us. It feels like an enormously long time before he speaks again.

"Tigers are beautiful creatures. So beautiful," he says. "There's even a poem about them. Listen. Tiger, Tiger, burning bright. Wish upon the first…tiger I see tonight."

"That's from two different poems," I tell him. "Or, a poem and a nursery rhyme, actually."

Chet shakes his head slowly, but doesn't say anything. He closes his eyes. He's still shaking his head when I turn to leave.

Outside, I feel disoriented. I start down the gravel driveway back to the street, but then turn around. I pick my way through the overgrown brush on the side of the house. I'm sure Chet or anyone else could see me if they looked out the window, but I don't care. I want to see the cage. Empty or not, I want to look into it and know what it was like for the thing inside.

Right away I can tell there's more to Rolson's mess of a backyard than can be seen by peeking through the Wengers' fence. In addition to the larger debris (threshers, cars, circus cage, etc.), there's a whole world of smaller artifacts hiding in the tall grass. There are rusted pop cans, some scattered haphazardly, others standing in a row like a miniature fence in front of a neglected lawn mower. There's a deflated kiddie pool. There's a half-length of garden hose. There's a man's boot with a bottle of hand lotion emerging from its top.

In one small section of the yard, not far from the house, the grass has been dug out. A menagerie of plastic toys sticks up from this raw patch of dirt. There are action figures—G.I. Joes and Ninja Turtles and some other characters I don't recognize, muscle-y cyborg-like things—buried to their waists, or, in some cases, to their necks. And there are animals. They're made of hard plastic and shaped like they are about to attack. These, too, are buried part way, but arranged in a semi-circle around the action figures as if standing guard, or poised to strike.

I puzzle over this display for some time. Is it the work of a child, angry and bored, burying his own possessions in the yard of his negligent, unpredictable parent? Or is it some art project undertaken by the father himself who, in a drug-addled state, and with no regard for the feelings of his son, wedged these toys into their current arrangement? I scan the animals for tigers, thinking their presence might prove something, one way or the other, but I see none. The closest I can find is a wolf. I bend down and pull it out of the dirt for closer inspection. It's a blue-gray color. Its jaws are open, and one paw, complete with tiny claws, is up, waiting to slash at whatever there is to slash. I realize right away this action is a mistake. Removing the wolf from the ground has broken the spell that's been over me since I first opened Rolson's door. I am suddenly acutely aware of where I am, of what I'm doing. I decide I do not actually need to see the cage at all. What I do need to do is get the hell off Rolson's property.

I set the wolf back into its original position in the dirt, but it looks all wrong there—skewed and obviously tampered with. Better that it be missing entirely than so clearly out of place. So I pick it up again, dust the soil off, and put it in my back pocket. Then I go.

I am trembling a little as I jog away from Rolson's and back down the street toward home. I keep my eyes on the ground, but after a moment, I am overtaken by the feeling of being watched. The sensation is so immediate, so visceral it stops me cold. I feel the tiny hairs along the ridge of my neck stand up—a most basic warning signal from the depths of my mammalian mind. Jenny is right; animals know when other animals are in trouble. There are, without a doubt, animal eyes upon me.

I lift my head, fearing the worst, the neighborhood nightmare come true.

But there's no tiger blocking my way. No creature of any sort stands in the middle of Derring Street.

The animal watching me has hidden itself beneath a cluster of patchy bushes that ring the Wengers' mailbox. These are feline eyes, yes, but small, surrounded by thin black fur and grown lazy from daily brushings and feedings. They belong to my own pet. Relief spills over me. I reach down and pull Boomer out from his hiding place. He doesn't resist. I carry him back home cradled in my arms. Jenny kisses me on the cheek and tells me I'm her hero.

Again, I think about apologizing to her, or saying "Okay, I'm ready to do what you want to do," or, at the very least, offering to call the police about Rolson. I think about showing her the wolf and telling her what I've seen— about the weirdness and sadness of the lives being lived just down the street from us. But I don't do any of these things and Jenny doesn't ask.

We're half way through summer now and whatever was making the sound is long gone, I'm convinced. It died or left or just folded up into itself and gave up on its sound-making. Sometimes I still catch Jenny listening for it, standing at the living room window, petting one or the other of the cats and looking pensive. I like to tease her about this by startling her from behind, or saying something inane like, "What's the matter, Jen? Tiger got your tongue?" She takes my kidding well.

Though I'd never admit it to Jenny, I am still listening for the sound, too. The cries may be gone, but the presence of the alleged tiger has never really left me. It stalks me from a safe distance, biding its time. I feel it most acutely in the thin hours of the morning and at dusk, when I'm walking down Derring Street into town, or out in the fields. Everywhere I go, something is amiss.

SPUD

SPUD II

July 15, 2090, Bainbridge Island, Washington
Caroline Olstead

At ten o'clock exactly, Angie pops into my toll booth with a cup of coffee in each hand, just like she has every Monday morning for the last two decades.

"I saw that little whore neighbor of yours at Starbucks," she says, setting one cup on the counter beside me and fishing a handful of sweetener packets from her pocket. "She was flirting with the boy at the register, holding up the whole line."

She's talking about Camden, Twila's daughter. I flick the switch under the counter, which sets the sign outside my booth to read "Lane Closed" in red neon. I am allowed to do this twice a day—fifteen minutes in the morning and sixty minutes at lunch.

"Better her hustling baristas for free scones than out at my place bothering Spud all day long," I say.

Camden's a year older than Spud and when they were little she was so sweet to him, almost like a big sister. Things changed though once the kids got closer to puberty, and these days… well, let's just say she's probably not the best influence in the world. But a crummy friend's better than no friend and that's what Spud would have otherwise. Once, I walked into his room to find the two of them on the bed, Camden's hand in Spud's shorts. They panicked and scrambled apart, but I just closed the door. None of my concern what two adolescents do.

"Does Spud even like girls?" Angie asks. "I never see him with people at all except you."

"He's not the social type," I say. "Just like his daddy, you remember? He'd rather read books, or hang around with cats and snakes. Spud's got this stray pit bull trained up to wait for him on our front steps all day. The thing's probably rabid. I keep telling him it's only a matter of time before the dog turns on him and then he'll be sorry. Can't trust pit bulls."

Angie puts the lid on her cup and says she ought to be getting back to her own booth. I thank her for the coffee and tell her I'll stop by before I go to lunch.

I've still got ten minutes left on my break, so I step out for a cigarette. We aren't allowed to smoke in our booths. I go over to the benches underneath the big green sign that says Bainbridge Island Bridge & Ferry Terminal.

The sign is a lie. There are no ferries anymore. Only the bridge, which was built in 2070 to connect the island to Seattle when the last tech boom hit and every brand new baby executive wanted a mansion in the woods, but still close to the city. The island's population tripled almost overnight. They were running two dozen ferries a day and the state built the bridge— ten miles long, a marvel of engineering—to accommodate all the extra traffic. A lot of town folks took toll jobs when it opened, Angie and myself included. But then when the bubble burst (whatever that means) nine years later and the economy turned bad, the state stopped running the ferries entirely. Now anyone who wants on or off the island has to cross the bridge, or drive their own boat. But who has the money for a boat anymore? No one, that's who.

At peak traffic times, I don't just take toll fares. I also have to ask drivers what's their purpose for leaving the island. If the answer isn't professional or medical, I can't allow them through. The state's rules, not mine, I tell them. With only one way off the island, the bridge can get overburdened quickly. Too many cars at once, and it becomes ten miles of parking lot. So it's only essential trips during rush hour, no exceptions. I had to remind Spud of that this very morning. He asked if we could go over to Seattle tonight, but I said no.

I don't feel too bad for the crossers I turn back. Everyone has had to make sacrifices since the market tanked. Some of us more than others. If it weren't for the bad economy, I wouldn't have Spud with me. This isn't to say I don't love my nephew (that's how I refer to him). I just mean things would have been a lot easier for both of us if he was able to stay where he belonged.

When the recession was at its worst, the University of Michigan lost funding for its genetics program and had to close down their whole kiddie-copy lab—couldn't even take care of what they'd made anymore. They called me one day out of the blue and said as next-of-kin I had to come get the boy. So I drove three days straight to pick up this two-year-old I'd never met, never even seen a picture of. Not that I didn't already know what he looked like. He looked just like Parker when Parker was two. There was a lot of paperwork, then this sophomore work-study nanny helped me strap him into a car seat and handed me a stack of files and a stuffed sea turtle she said was the boy's favorite thing in the world. She had tears in her eyes when she waved goodbye to us and then there I was with this toddler. I was so totally unprepared to have him in my life. A lot of the time, I still feel unprepared. We drove back to Washington with him babbling to his turtle the whole way. Sweet kid. He had Parker's giant, oblong head, squinty brown eyes, and straight hair on top. I couldn't help but call him Spud.

Potato Head. Parker Potato. When we were kids, my little brother dubbed me Carrie Carrot for spite, but I said it didn't work that way since my head looked nothing like a carrot. When mom would hear me call him Parker Potato, she'd say, "Don't be cruel." But she thought Spud was all right, and after a while it was the only name either of us ever used for him.

This one, too, just the same. Spud, too. Spud two. Spud, also. No one calls him Parker, which is for the best I think. Being a junior is hard, especially when you've never met the senior. So he's Spud at home, Spud at school, Spud at church.

Spud will never know he's a clone and neither will anyone else. I made that promise to myself from the beginning. The University of Michigan clone program got a lot of press when it first started, none of it good. And since the lab closed, Spud's peers from Ann Arbor haven't fared well on the whole. The families who've been open about their children's origins have taken a lot of flak. Just six months ago, there was a story in the news about a little clone girl who got her skull bashed in by a boy from her school. He hit her with a bat while others cheered him on. These days it's fine to be gay or handicapped or pretty much any weird religion, but Lord help a kid if he's a biological double of another human being. They're the new schoolyard pariahs, clones are. As if the boy doesn't take enough abuse already just for being himself.

When Spud asks about his daddy, I tell him stories about how he was an American hero.

When Spud asks about his mother, I say, "That's none of your concern."

It's hard, me being the only family the boy's got. Sometimes, I worry I'm not enough. I mean, he was supposed to be raised in a state-of-the-art lab with top teachers and high-tech accommodations. All I've got to offer him here on Bainbridge is a dinky old house and crummy, crumbling public schools. Money is tight. I can't even afford things like summer camps and book-of-the-month clubs for him. And Lord knows I'm no great intellectual role model myself. Spud's already past the point in school where I can be of much help on his homework, even if he wanted it.

I think about all of this while I smoke my cigarette under that lie of a sign. What's got me going on this whole train of thought, aside from Angie's remarks, is that today is Spud's birthday. His thirteenth. He wanted me to take him to the natural history museum in the city. What kind of kid wants to go to a museum for his birthday? Spud, of course. But, like I said, I had to tell him no. It'll be rush hour by the time I get off work, and, birthday or no birthday, you need a damn good reason to cross the bridge at rush hour.

The best I can do for him today is cake and candles. Except even in that, I'm falling short. We're out of eggs and milk, both of which I'll need for the cake. I call Spud to see if he can run down to the store to get some, but he doesn't pick up his phone, which means his hands are busy doing God-knows-what.

End
Times

The apocalypse will begin with a series of beeps. Not like an alarm clock or a smoke detector. More like the sound of a truck backing up: patient, but persistent. I know this the same way you know the address of your parents' house or the color of the walls in your childhood bedroom—I've been there before and retained the salient details.

I won't personally make it to this apocalypse, however. My death is slated for a day in June 2031, a little over a year before the big event. While jogging around the indoor track at a 24 Hour Fitness in downtown Seattle, I'll suffer an aneurysm and collapse. I'll be dead before my face hits the spongy rubber floor. I will be forty-seven years old.

The fact of my own death will come as such a non-surprise to me that I'll fail to warn Cole of its imminence.[1] This is ironic because from the time my son is old enough to understand words, I'll routinely remind him that the world will end before his sixteenth birthday.

"So, best not to take life too seriously, sweetheart," I'll say.

Cole will not heed my advice. He'll be an honors student, captain of his Knowledge Bowl team, and an active participant in Amnesty International for Kids. He'll be a chronic worrier. A sloucher, a brow furrower, and a bit of a hypochondriac. This is to say Cole will take after his mother.

Would I rather see Cole spend his life as some pint-sized hedonist—apathetic, uninvolved, unconcerned, only interested in cheap thrills and the trappings of his own abbreviated youth? Certainly not. What I'll mean when I tell Cole not to take life too seriously is that this show—this right here, right now—isn't the only show there is. And as caught up as we get in ourselves, these selves are so very very temporary that it almost isn't worth paying them

---

1 Or, maybe "fail" is the wrong word. Maybe "choose not to" is better. After all, some conversations are just plain undesirable, no matter many opportunities I'm given to have them. I feel guilty about this. Although there's nothing to be done about it now—Cole won't be born for another four years. The man I'm currently sitting across from at this coffee shop isn't the man who will be Cole's father, so no use asking him for help. I suppose I could write myself a note: Tell Cole you will die young. I mean it this time!! But I know it wouldn't make any difference and Cole will still wind up unprepared. This isn't pessimistic conjecture on my part. When I say I know, you must believe me. I know.

much attention at all. I'll want him to strive for a degree of non-attachment. Of course, I don't know why I'll think it's reasonable to ask this of my child when I've never been much good at it myself. No matter how many times I've tried.

Cole's father Aaron will never express any particular concern over my warnings. As an acquisitions editor for a small but respectable publishing house and therefore a man with a keen appreciation for literary device, Aaron will take this apocalypse-forecasting as allegory. He'll assume my prophecies function in much the same way other adults use the story of Santa Claus to ensure good behavior in their children. Aaron will be inclined to overlook other faults of mine as well. And I his. We'll be tremendously fond of one another in that fault-overlooking sort of way. In this respect, Cole will do us both good. He'll be our harshest critic. From the time he is very young, his honesty will be unwavering, unclouded by his affections.[2]

The last time I'll see Cole alive (or, more accurately, the last time Cole will see me alive), he'll be sitting at the kitchen table, working on the final project for his math class. His glasses will have slipped down almost to the tip of his nose. I'll resist the urge to reach out and push them back up. At fourteen, he will be fiercely opposed to that sort of motherly intervention.

"Cole, maybe it's time to knock this stuff off for a bit. Wouldn't you rather go play video games? Or smoke a joint? Or have unprotected sex with one of the neighbor girls?" I'll say.

"I have to get an A in Mr. Ferguson's class if I want him to recommend me for honors geometry next year."

"Maybe honors geometry isn't the most important thing in the world," I'll remind him, taking a bottle of water from the fridge and zipping it into my gym bag.

"It is to me," Cole will say.

A week later, and five days after my funeral, he'll graduate from the eighth grade at the top of his class. He'll wear the same suit for both occasions.

---

2 For this, I love him already.

A sure sign that an apocalypse is on its way[3]—well before the beeping picks up—is violent and repeated movement of continental plates. There are earthquakes and volcanic eruptions. There are tsunamis. Mountains get taller and canyons get deeper. The Galapagos Islands double in number. Not all of these tectonic shifts are catastrophic, and they don't all happen at once. In fact, it usually takes several weeks for the news media to begin suggesting the Earth is experiencing anything out of the ordinary.

This time around, the first pre-apocalypse tremor to ripple along the Cascadia Fault will coincide with the first day of Cole's sophomore year of high school. As treasurer of the West Seattle High School Safety Committee, Cole will clearly and calmly instruct his peers in French II to take cover under their desks until the shaking subsides. He will then lead the class (his befuddled, French-born teacher included) out of the building to the twenty-yard-line of the football stadium where they will have been previously instructed to line up during disaster preparedness drills. The earthquake will register a 4.1 on the Richter scale with its epicenter off the coast of Vancouver Island. No one at West Seattle High will suffer any injury as a result of the incident and school will not be dismissed early that day, despite the wishes of Cole's peers. Cole himself will not have strong feelings about this one way or the other.

Ten days later, Mount Hood and Mount Jefferson will erupt within six hours of one another. The news stations will report a reasonable amount of panic in Oregon, but outside of the state reactions will be demure, speculative. *Better them than us* will be the general response from Washingtonians who will look wearily in the directions of their own

---

3 How many apocalypses have there been? I don't know. I myself have experienced seven. If I had to guess though, I would say there have been infinite apocalypses. It seems the universe is stuck in a never-ending loop of creating and destroying itself. With each re-creation, the universe is reborn more or less the same as the previous version. The end doesn't always come at the same point in time though. The last apocalypse took place in the fall of 1997. I was eating a bag of Sun Chips and watching Boy Meets World when it happened. I remember turning the volume on the TV up as high as it would go in an effort to drown out that horrible beeping.

As far as I can tell, there's no rhyme or reason to when a given incarnation of the world will end. One time, the apocalypse might happen in 2074, the next time in 1812. I'm aware that whole worlds have begun and ended without me ever having existed. Not every Earth lasts long enough to see my birth in 1984. This is fine with me. I don't mind sitting one out every now and then.

volcanoes. It will take less than twenty-four hours for ash plumes to reach Seattle.

The Sunday afternoon ash begins to fall like rain, Cole and Aaron will stand on the front porch together, taking in the spectacle. Cole will pull the collar of his t-shirt up over his mouth and nose.

"We shouldn't stay outside too long," he'll say, his voice muffled. "There's a heightened risk of developing respiratory inflammation from breathing in all this foreign matter. Prolonged exposure might even result in chronic asthma."

"I don't think we're really breathing ash into our lungs," Aaron will say. "Isn't that what our nose hairs are for?"

"It's not the ash itself that's the problem. Ash is just pulverized rock. It's all the other stuff that comes along with the ash, the bacteria that hitches a ride on the ash. That's what we've really got to worry about."

"It that true?" Aaron will ask.

"Eighty percent certain. I'll look into it."

Then father and son will go back inside—back to reading separate books in their separate bedrooms, as will be their weekend custom.

"Do you think there will be more earthquakes?" Cole will ask, appearing at Aaron's door sometime later.

"I don't know. You're the science expert here, not me. Do _you_ think there will be more earthquakes?"

"I think there's a good chance, yes."

"If your mom was here, she would say this is a sign," Aaron will muse.

"Well, technically, everything's a sign of something," Cole will say. "I mean, everything's a cause of something, if you believe in the butterfly effect. Or nothing is a sign of anything, if you believe in David Hume."

"And which do you believe in?"

"I'll tell you what I believe. I believe we should get a proper earthquake kit. First aid supplies, blankets, flashlights, portable radio, iodine tablets, three days worth of food."

Aaron will give Cole twenty dollars and tell him he can start by stocking up on canned goods from the corner store. Cole will accept this mission with enthusiasm.[4]

Despite having been raised by devout Jewish parents, Aaron will never consider himself a spiritual person. But following the earthquake and the eruptions, he will begin to look for explanations beyond himself. It will start with a conversation with a man in a robe downtown. The man will be bearded; his robe will be dirty and frayed at the hem. The man will be proselytizing, but he won't speak to Aaron directly when he passes. Aaron, on his lunch break the day after the ash first arrives, will approach the man unbidden. Aaron will listen as the man talks about goodness, and grace, and love for all sentient creatures, and the life that comes after this one. He will give Aaron three sticks of incense and a Xeroxed pamphlet of prayers in a language Aaron won't recognize. There are transliterations on the back of each page, the man will explain.

When Aaron gets home that night, Cole will still be at school, tied up with some extracurricular activity or another. Aaron will take off his suit jacket and brush the ash out of his hair into the kitchen sink. In the first days after the eruptions, it will be impossible to spend more than a few minutes outside without the volcanic residue collecting on any uncovered extremities.

Aaron will pull the incense and prayer booklet from his briefcase and sit cross-legged on the living room floor, spreading the items out on the coffee table. He'll follow the robed man's instructions, lighting each stick and circling the air around it with his right hand, as if beckoning the smoke upward to God. This is how the man will have said it, *beckoning the smoke upward to God*. Aaron will read the foreign prayers out loud, placing each incense stick on an individual saucer (for lack of proper holders).

In this action, he will feel little goodness, or grace, or love for all sentient

---

4 I can picture this so clearly, it's almost like I'm there with Cole. Or like I am him, in a way. I can feel the chill of the fall air against his arms as he walks to the store. I can feel the weight of the cans and bottles in his hands as he lifts them from the shelves. This is too close. This is not information a mother should have access to. Yet, at the same time, it seems right and natural. I wish I could better explain how time and personhood are not fixed or concrete at all. We walk around thinking we are one person in one place at one time, but this is not really the case. Except when it is the case. Which is most of the time, for most people. Just not for me. What makes me so special? I can't even begin to speculate.

Though it's currently August, the chill from Cole's walk to the store has given me goose bumps. I wrap my arms around myself. My boyfriend asks, "Are you cold?" As if anyone could actually be cold drinking coffee indoors in August. He tells me he's got a jacket in his car I can wear. I tell him no, I'm fine. This feeling will pass in a moment.

creatures. Instead, he'll feel slightly foolish. He'll try to imagine what I might say if I could see him. He'll decide I'd approve, if for no other reason than his appearance with the incense makes an amusing spectacle. [5]

Similarly, he'll know that Cole's response won't be so accepting. When Aaron hears the front door open, he'll grab for his briefcase, push the whole mess on the coffee table into it, close the case, and stand to greet his son.

"It smells like smoke in here," Cole will say.

"It smells like smoke everywhere," Aaron will say. Cole will accept this answer. Then he will carefully shake free the ash from his hair into a Tupperware container. He'll shut himself in his room and examine that same ash under his compound microscope until Aaron tells him it's time to eat.

From his observations of the ash he collects, Cole will assemble an entry for his school's fall science fair. On poster board, he will diagram the way ash does in fact pick up bacteria and other microorganisms as it moves hundreds of miles from the eruption site to places beyond. His project will win first prize for his grade and the honor of competing in a regional contest in Wenatchee at the end of the semester. This contest will never actually take place, of course.

The second symptom of an impending end-of-the-world is that the moon speeds up. Instead of completing a circuit around our planet once every 27.2 days, it gradually moves faster and faster until people see a full moon on an almost weekly basis. The most concerning side effect from the moon's acceleration is a corresponding acceleration of the Earth's tides. Where the tide normally comes in and goes out twice a day, once the apocalypse nears, it instead comes in and goes out upwards of seven times in a twenty-four-hour period. This is extremely disruptive to the planet's

---

[5] Aaron and I will be pretty good at anticipating one another's reactions in most situations. After all, we've already known each other for most of our lives. Or most of my life, rather. There's a bit of an age difference—almost a decade between us. We grew up living mere blocks from one another. The first time I saw Aaron, I was five years old and riding the bus in Everett with my grandma. As soon as we boarded, I spotted a group of teenagers near the back. I pointed to the slightest among them. "Someday you and me are going to get married," I told him. This was Aaron. The other boys laughed and Grandma apologized on my behalf, but Aaron was a good sport. "Sounds like a plan," he said, flashing me a thumbs up. After that, he'd wave whenever he saw me around. This waving continued for a number of years, until he left for college.

ocean life, and many of the creatures that dwell close to the shore beach themselves out of confusion. To unsuspecting observers, it may appear as if the sea is literally belching up its inhabitants, forcibly expelling them from their watery homes.

The morning fish, mollusks, and several small sharks begin to wash up along Alki Beach, Cole will be getting ready for school, drinking instant coffee with the TV turned to the morning news. When he sees the news report, he will take Aaron's car (though he'll only have his learner's permit and not a real driver's license) and drive to the shore. He will stand beside the newsmen, the baffled lifeguards, and the team of marine biologists from the University of Washington and survey the scene. Then he will return home to gather up all the plastic tubs and buckets he can find. He will change into his Boy Scout uniform because he will feel the outfit lends him some air of authority. He will drive back to the beach and begin collecting sea creatures from the sand, one per tub or bucket, which he will first fill with seawater. No one will interfere with his activities.

Back at the house, Cole will transfer the larger creatures to sinks and bathtubs, each with a rubber stopper jammed tight over the drain. The smaller fish will stay in their buckets for the time being, placed in a neat row below the living room window so they can enjoy some natural light. Despite his often cold approach to other people, my son will always have a soft spot for animals. He'll always make it his mission to rescue any pets lost in our neighborhood, and he'll insist each year that one of his Hanukkah presents be a donation to the Humane Society. Still, that Cole would skip school and violate traffic laws to resuscitate half-dead sea slugs will come as a surprise to Aaron. And a little bit to Cole himself, although he won't admit it.[6]

---

6 It's an experience I'm glad Cole will get to have this time around. Obviously, when the apocalypse doesn't happen during his fifteenth year, Cole's teens go a little differently. His whole life goes a little differently. Everyone's does, except for mine. In these instances, I still always cash out at the gym on the same day in June. But there are some versions of the world where Aaron too gets to see his life to its natural end—a stroke shortly after his eighty-second birthday. Cole goes, along with his wife, a decade later in a single-engine plane crash, orphaning their twin sons. Since I never meet my grandchildren, the grief they must feel does not weigh so heavily on me. As adults, they go on to co-own a successful toy store in Missoula, Montana.

Of course, no one remembers any of this from one apocalypse to the next. No one, except me. A gift and a curse. Live enough of the present and you get to see into the future. Although I'll admit, after this many times around, it's hard to separate memory from premonition.

"Your mother would be pleased to see you showing some spontaneity," Aaron will tell Cole that evening as they wait for dinner to arrive. They will have to order pizza because the baby sixgill shark in the kitchen sink will make cooking difficult.

"Let's not talk about that," Cole will say.

"What should we talk about?"

"Saltwater. And hydrometers and filtration systems. Aquariums, in essence. The fish are all right for now, but they can only sit in stagnant water for so long. They'll need proper accommodations if they're going to survive."

Aaron will nod. Always supportive, always understanding. "And how long will your new friends be staying with us, do you think?"

"Until it's safe for them to go back to the ocean."

"Cole, I'm not sure things are ever going to go back to normal."

"The Earth is in a constant state of flux," Cole will say. "Sure, something is happening now that's different than what we're used to, but that's just the risk of living on a dynamic planet. You've got to expect change. In a few years, we'll be looking at different scenarios entirely. The thing to remember is that nothing is permanent."

"Your mother would be happy to hear you say that, too."

"I thought we were talking about something else."

Aaron will agree to take Cole to get tanks, filters, fish food, multi-colored rocks, tiny plastic castles, and whatever else his son thinks their aquatic refugees may need. Aaron and Cole will have to drive to a strip mall in the University District to buy their supplies since the aquarium and terrarium store near the house will have closed without explanation. It's not hard to infer explanation though. No sign necessary to say where the owners will have gone. To someplace else. Hoping, despite news reports insisting otherwise, that only the Pacific Northwest is in turmoil.

Back home, Aaron and Cole will set up a dozen tanks and fish bowls. The sea creatures will seem content enough in their new homes with the exception of a fist-sized octopus, which sometime during the night will open the top of its tank and climb out. In the morning, Cole will discover the animal splayed out flat on the hardwood floor, not dead but clearly unwell. Cole's solution to the octopus-escape-problem will be constant vigilance. He'll return the octopus to its original bucket and keep that bucket with him at all times.

What comes next is the distortion of night and day. In Seattle, for example, the sun rises at six in the morning, then sets shortly thereafter. Then it rises again at noon. And so on and so forth. This is because the Earth, like the moon before it, has sped up in its rotation—both on its axis and around the sun. My best guess about this is that basically an apocalypse is just the whole universe spinning into itself. These stages are all about picking up speed.

On his way to class each morning, Cole, wearing his Boy Scout jersey, will stop at a nearby elementary school to act as crossing guard. Octopus bucket in one hand and a bright orange flag in the other, he'll escort younger kids—those whose parents are still sending them to school—across California Avenue.

"It's not safe for them to be walking around in the street in the dark," he'll explain to Aaron.

Aaron will agree, but he'll wonder why this responsibility should fall to his son. He'll also wonder if perhaps someone shouldn't be looking out for Cole in the dark as well. This will be the first time in a long time that Aaron will think to be concerned for Cole's safety. Usually, Cole will be sufficiently concerned for his own safety that Aaron need not bother.

The following week, a series of small earthquakes will once again rattle the Puget Sound region. Geologists will debate whether these tremors are aftershocks from the first quake six weeks ago, or independent seismic movement.[7] For the most part, these quakes will be so slight that they require no real response on the part of those who feel them. In a growing list of environmental concerns, they will barely register. So what if the breakfast dishes rattle a bit? Once the shaking subsides, Cole will give a quick glance into the bucket by his feet and go right on back to eating his oatmeal like nothing's happened.

Across the kitchen, assembling brown bag lunches, Aaron, too, will look to the octopus.

---

7 Of course, no movement is ever independent. The geologists will know this. Newton taught us that every action has an equal and opposite reaction. Has there ever been a more true observation? Look, I can bounce my leg against one end of the table in front of me and at the other side my boyfriend's coffee splashes about in its cup, his scone threatens to tip off its plate. "Could you not do that?" he asks. Then he picks up the scone and takes a bite. My point? The world's creation ensures its eventual destruction. And that destruction ensures its eventual re-creation. So yes, the earthquakes are connected, both in the sense that all earthquakes have always been connected, and also in the more immediate sense as well.

"Does your octopus have a name?" he'll ask Cole.

"No. Naming animals, especially wild, non-domesticated animals, is an act of pointless sentimentality. Why would I give something a name when it doesn't even care if I call to it or not? It can't respond. It has no knowledge of itself as an individual. What does something like that need with a name?"

"You should give your octopus a name."

"Tell me one good reason why it needs a name and I'll give it one."

"Because it's cumbersome to always have to refer to the two of you as 'Cole and his octopus in a bucket.' Like if some of your friends from school were to come by and you weren't home, I would have say, 'Cole and his octopus in a bucket are out right now, but they'll be back soon.' You see what I mean?"

"I don't really have friends from school who come by the house looking for me."

"Please name the octopus, Cole."

"If anyone from school wants to find me, which they rarely do, they can just call my phone. I don't see your scenario as being all that plausible."

"How about something alliterative, like Oscar the Octopus, or Olin the Octopus?"

"Oliver."

"Good."

That night, a Friday night, Aaron will go to temple. He won't tell Cole where he's going. Cole, absorbed in a book about continental drift, will take little notice of his father's absence. Or if he does, he won't remark on it. Although he will use the opportunity to sneak a chunk of cheddar cheese to Oliver.

"What the hell, Ollie," Cole will whisper. "You only go around once."

At the synagogue, Aaron will sit in the back with a bound prayer book open on his lap. He'll take comfort in the weight of the book and the sound of familiar words he's never known the meaning of. He can count on his fingers the number of Hebrew words he understands: "yes," "please," "sorry," "no," "blessed-art-thou," and five names for God.

The room will be filled to capacity. It will occur to Aaron that others, like him, may be drawn in such times of uncertainty to faith. Or if not to faith, to familiar words and weighty texts. To the safety of traditions remembered from childhood—when to stand, when to sit, twisting hands through the fringes of father's prayer shawl to pass the time while the grown-ups chant out a senseless melody, not beautiful but lulling, then grape juice and cookies after *kiddush*, followed by a sleepy car ride home.

The rabbi will resist the obvious temptation to proselytize on the situation at hand and its possible correlations to the vengeful God of the Torah. Aaron will appreciate this. And though he'll want to glean meaning from the sermon, Aaron will have trouble connecting to the rabbi's words in English and wish he could have slipped out once the Hebrew prayers concluded. His mind will wander. After services, he'll leave quickly.

Walking though the parking lot, Aaron will pause, involuntarily, a few yards from his car, overcome by the feeling that he is about to fall. He'll worry he's going to tip forward, or perhaps backward. For a panicky moment, he will lose all sense of bearing and grounding. He'll bend over, grabbing his knees for support until the feeling passes. This will be a problem of gravity— or rather, the illusion of a change in gravity. With the planet accelerating, objects on Earth will feel at times unmoored. Momentarily lighter, or heavier, or simply off-kilter. It is not uncommon during this stage for people to suffer a periodic sense of disorder and disorientation—as if they are no longer connected to the planet's surface in quite the same way as before.

Back home, Cole will have switched from reading to scouring the Internet for information on North American subduction zones. The octopus bucket will sit on the desk beside the computer, a single curious tentacle probing along the edge of the container. Without looking away from the screen, Cole will gently coax the tentacle back into the water. "Easy, boy," he'll say. Aaron, seeking distraction, will offer to play cards or a board game with his son. Cole will decline.

On Saturday morning, Aaron will wake feeling unwell. The sensation of being off-balance will have returned to him. In addition to that, an intermittent but severe nausea. At the breakfast table, he'll notice that Cole has only just picked at the toast in front of him. When he asks Cole if he's feeling all right, his son will give no more response than a dismissive nod. Aaron will try to eat a slice of Cole's neglected toast with little success, his stomach turning, tongue seemingly too fat, his teeth too small.

He'll suggest to Cole that the two of them go together to visit my grave. This is something they'll have done only once since my death—for the unveiling of my headstone. Otherwise, both my husband and son will avoid the sprawling cemetery. Although they will never discuss it with one another, they'll both hold the belief that there is nothing really left of me at Washington Memorial Park.

But in his increasing anxiety, Aaron will continue to seek tangible reassurances. A grave is indeed the most tangible reminder of the dead. And so for this, I cannot fault him.[8]

"Bring Ollie," Aaron will say to Cole, hoping to make the outing more palatable.

Cole, already dressed in a suit and tie, will beg off claiming a prior obligation: a Security Council meeting for his Model United Nations club.

"I can't just ditch with no explanation," he'll say.

"Visiting your mother's grave isn't a valid explanation?"

"Sure, if I had cleared it with the Secretary General when we set the meeting schedule. But at the time, I assured my fellow delegates I had no personal conflicts on this date. It would be unprofessional for me to cancel at the last minute for a non-emergency situation. Are you saying this is an emergency situation?"

Aaron will want to tell his son that with the Earth shifting beneath them, night and day blurring into one, and a host of displaced sea creatures residing in the living room, every situation is, in fact, an emergency situation.

Instead, he'll offer Cole a ride to school. On the way, they'll watch the sun sink low in the sky with alarming speed. When they arrive, Aaron will be tempted to kiss Cole on the cheek, but he'll restrain himself. As Cole gets out

---

8 I should mention that today is the day Aaron and I meet. Or re-meet as adults. In fact, he's already here.

My boyfriend and I come to this coffee shop every Sunday morning. It's our routine. We bring a newspaper, books, journals, whathaveyou, and camp out in a pair of armchairs by a large south-facing window. We usually stay until noon, then we pack up and go elsewhere, sometimes together, sometimes separately. More often than not it's been separately, as of late. I try not to worry too much about this, considering that in a month's time, I'm going to leave him for another man.

Aaron got here about an hour ago. He's working on his laptop at a table across the room, with his back to us. But every so often he turns to look in this direction. He still appears very much like the kid with the skateboard I propositioned more than two decades ago, only taller now, shoulders broader, etc. In a few minutes, my boyfriend will get up to go to the restroom and Aaron will take the opportunity to come over. "Excuse me, I know this sounds lame," he'll say, "but you look so familiar. Have we met before?" I'll say yes, but I won't remind him of the bus, only that I recognize him from the old neighborhood. "Well, it's good to see you again," he'll say. Nothing more than that. But in the coming weeks, we'll cross paths several more times. And like the old days, we'll wave each time. Until Aaron works up the nerve to ask me out.

of the car, Aaron will hand him his book bag, then his octopus bucket, and wish him good luck in his international negotiations.

In the day's second twilight, Aaron will pick through the cemetery with uncertain steps. Because my death will be sudden and early, Aaron and I will have made no prior preparations. In hindsight, Aaron will wish we'd had plans. As it is, I'll be wedged between two unfamiliar dead people and Aaron will spend the bulk of his cemetery visit looking around for open plots, wondering, if he died that very day, how close in the ground could he get to me?[9]

Aaron won't bring flowers to my grave. Instead, he'll bring seven small rocks, pilfered from the neighbors' Zen garden. It's a tradition in the Jewish faith to leave pebbles when visiting the dead, harkening back to days when the ancient Israelites rolled boulders over graves, either to keep animals out or spirits in. On this point, religious scholars are uncertain. Aaron won't give the origins of the tradition much consideration. For him, it will be a way to show his grieving has not yet ended. He'll take the rocks out of his pocket and line them, one by one, across the top of my headstone. As soon as he's done this, Aaron will feel overcome by dizziness. It will seem to him as if the world below him is literally spinning, as if the rules governing planet Earth have betrayed him and he may at any moment slip from its face and fly off into the air. It will be similar to the way he felt in the synagogue parking lot, but this time, much, much worse. He'll drop to his knees and press his palms to the recently watered grass, trying to regain balance. The problem, he'll decide, is a matter of weight. He'll remove the rocks from my headstone in the reverse order from how he set them down and return them to his pocket. The spinning will subside and Aaron will stand up. But in its wake, the sensation will linger. He'll stop looking around for vacant plots. Instead, on his way back to his car, Aaron will keep an eye out for pebbles, bending to pocket them each time he sees one.

---

9 Believe me, I know this feeling, this want to always, always be with the ones I love. Even as I am, at this moment, preparing to meet Aaron, I am also preparing to lose him. Although the universe's incarnations may be infinite, my time within said universe is not. I haven't always been here. And I won't always be here. In fact, this universe is my last go-around. I find no relief in this knowledge (which, again, I know just as you know all things familiar and inevitable to you). Just the opposite. I hate to think that this is the last time I'll marry Aaron on the shore of Lake Washington, the last time I'll hold Cole, pink and angry and new on the day of his birth, each moment spent alongside my husband and son the last of that moment. I would gladly keep going on like this with them forever.

At home, Aaron will sit cross-legged on the living room floor in front of the coffee table just as he did the evening after he met the holy man in the robe. He will take the rocks from his pocket and set them in a row across the coffee table. Then another row of rocks along the arm of the sofa. Somehow, this will feel right: to weigh down our household objects and undo the effects of what he believes is Earth's new gravity upon them. Or perhaps it's to grieve for them. For the life the three of us shared in their presence. Aaron won't know for certain the reason, only that the action is important in that moment. He'll go once again to collect rocks from the neighbors' neglected Zen garden. These particular neighbors—the McEwans—will have moved out a number of weeks before to join family in Minneapolis. In fact, most of the block will have left for places away from fault lines and volcanoes, away from the coast. Aaron will take his time putting rocks on each piece of furniture, across doorframes, along windowsills, returning to the McEwans' yard as needed.

When Cole gets home, Aaron won't try to hide what he's doing. In fact, he won't even look up from his task to greet his son until he runs out of rocks and has to go next door for more. Cole will stand in the doorway and watch as Aaron gathers a double handful of pebbles. He'll continue to watch as Aaron finishes with that batch and goes to fetch another. Only then will Cole stop him, pressing his hand against his father's chest as he tries to pass.

"This will go quicker if we bring all the rocks inside at once," Cole will say.

He'll take two garbage bags and go out to the McEwans' yard and fill them to carrying capacity. He'll drag the bags one by one back into the house. Then he'll set about helping his father line every surface of our modest home with rocks.

When I think about him doing this, I am filled with pride, more so even than when I think of him rescuing sea creatures, or shepherding grade school children across darkened streets.[10]

---

10 And in thinking of this, I've started to tear up a little. I wipe at my eyes with the sleeve of my sweater. My boyfriend looks at me over his newspaper. "What's wrong?" he asks. I can't tell him. "Sad thoughts," I say. He shakes his head. We've been together four months and, though he'd never say it, he's already tired of this behavior—my unexplained shifts in mood, my detachment, my clinging, my crying. I'm all over the place these days. "Let me run to the restroom and get you some paper towels," he offers. It's the best he can do. The most he's willing to do. He folds the newspaper and tucks it under his arm as he goes. Across the room, Aaron turns to look at me once more, stands, pushes in his chair, and takes his first step toward me.

Cole will remove his jacket and roll up the sleeves of his dress shirt, tie thrown over his right shoulder. He'll join Aaron in arranging the rocks. He'll set them across radiators. He'll set them on the keyboard and printer. He'll set them on family photographs. He'll slip them into medicine cabinets and dresser drawers. He'll make his bed and put three rocks on his pillow. He'll create neat circles of rocks around each burner on the stove. One rock on top of every spice in the spice rack. Cole will place rocks on the shelves of bookcases and along the rims of each fish tank. He'll drop a handful into Oliver's bucket. Then he'll crawl on hands and knees toward his father. Aaron will be sitting on the floor, legs splayed out to one side, laying rocks along the baseboards in the living room. It will be slow going. When he reaches Aaron, Cole will take a rock from Aaron's pile and balance it near the ankle of the older man's left leg. Aaron will not notice. Cole will set another rock beside it. Then another. The line of rocks will creep up Aaron's calf. Aaron will stop his own work to watch his son's progress. Aaron will smile at his son who will in turn smile back. Is this a ritual or a game? Mourning or play? Aaron will try to think of something to say to solidify this moment—something they can both refer back to in the future. But nothing will come. He will feel the spinning sensation again and have to lie down, careful not to disturb Cole's rocks on his leg. Unbidden, Cole will lie beside him, piling rocks along his own torso, from sternum to belt buckle.

That's when the beeping will start.

SPUD

SPUD II

July 15, 2090, Bainbridge Island, Washington
Parker Timothy Olstead II

The dog follows him down to the beach. The morning is a thick fog and he can barely see through to the water. The beach has no sand, just rocks and he sits cross-legged, searching out the bigger rocks around him and pitching them into the water. He pretends the world's rock supply is out of balance—too many on land and not enough underwater. It's his job to correct the problem, to even things out for the good of all Earth's creatures. He likes when the rocks land too far out in the fog for him to see the splash. He just has to trust the sound. The dog lies by his side, waiting.

He believes the dog is his father. He believes the apple tree in the front yard is his mother. He has read that Buddhists say their parents are infinite. Plants, animals, rocks, air—these things are all parents. He does not actually take any comfort in the idea, but he wants to. He reads a lot, checking out as many books as he's allowed from the molding public library. He is trying on different theories and concepts, looking to see what fits. He knows Catholics believe in one god split up into three parts. He knows sometimes Hindus burn their dead along the banks of the river Ganges. He knows at thirteen, a boy in the Jewish faith is considered a man. He wants very much to be a man. He feels like he's ready for that. Not that he wants to be bigger, or stronger, or to live on his own. What he thinks of when he thinks of being a man is to be free of his childish needs: his squirming, nervous desire to be loved; his orphan's remorse; his constant wondering about who his parents were, what were they like, and what would they think of him. He's thirteen now, and he vows to be a man—to be done with all that. After all, his father is a dog. His mother is an apple tree. What more could a man need?

Behind him, he hears the crunch of sandals over rocks. He looks and it's Camden, gnawing on a big chocolate chip cookie, the kind they sell at the coffee shop. He turns back to the water, half hoping she'll pass by without stopping to talk to him, half hoping she won't.

"Do you know what a blowjob is, Spud?" Camden asks. She has paused directly behind him, with one knee bent so it's pressing between his shoulder blades.

"Yes."

"Do you want me to give you one?"

"No."

"Then you must not know what one is. If you knew what one was, you wouldn't say 'no.' Everybody who knows what blowjobs are wants one. All the time, all anyone wants is blowjobs once they know. This is why you're no good at school. Too dumb to admit when you don't know something."

"I'm just fine at school."

"Your aunt told my mom you get terrible grades. And you have no friends."

"My aunt and your mom can go fuck each other."

At school, the kids call him Crater Head. They say, "Your daddy saw your ugly head and was so sad he drove his rocket into a black hole." They ask, "Did your daddy die because he crashed into your giant face?" "When you were born, did your mother get sucked up your nose?" At home, his aunt says, "Don't mind them, Spud, kids are always cruel," then she goes next door to spend all her time with Twila. Once, he walked into her room to find the two of them on the bed, Caroline's hand up Twila's skirt. They'd panicked and scrambled apart, but he'd just closed the door. None of his concern what two grown women do.

"If you let me give you a blowjob, I'll show you something about your dad," Camden says, kneeling beside him. Sometimes Spud is certain she is the devil, come to waylay all his plans as soon as he makes them. He wants to stay strong in his resolve not to dwell on his parents any longer. He wants to tell her he doesn't care in the slightest.

"What about my dad?"

"Your aunt's got files in our house. One of the files has your dad's name on it."

"His name's the same as my name."

"Your name's Lieutenant Colonel Olstead?"

He doesn't say anything. He finds a flat rock under his knee and throws it into the water. Camden leans closer. He can smell the cookie on her breath. She should have at least offered to share it with him, he thinks. It's his birthday, after all.

"It looks important," she says. "A big important file. It might have your mom's name in it, too."

Camden's got her hand on the fly of his jeans. She undoes the button and slips her fingers over the top of his boxer shorts. Her hand feels cold and damp, like she's part of the fog.

"Show me the file, then we'll do what you want," he says.

Katie Eats Boston Cream Pie at a Motel Diner in Southeast Portland

The people in the room next door are fucking. Katie hears not just the moans and the squeaking bedsprings, but other things too like the rubbing of thighs, the biting of ears, and the clenching of starchy sheets between fists. It's nights like these, Katie wishes she was an astronaut.

This wish has nothing to do with the people next door.

Katie's cell phone rings and it's Darryl. She doesn't answer. She doesn't want Darryl to think she's in the kind of place where people are fucking and she can hear it.

It occurs to her that she probably doesn't really hear the clenching of starchy sheets between fists, probably not the ear biting and thigh rubbing as well. Those parts, she's imagining. Probably. But she can hear a lot. She worries Darryl would be able to hear a lot too, over the phone. "Are you okay?" he'd ask.

He'd ask that anyway, but if he heard the fucking, he'd ask with a different inflection. And also "Where are you right now?" And also "When are you coming back?"

He'd ask those things anyway too. Katie decides the fucking actually has little bearing on what Darryl would say. The fucking is not the reason Katie doesn't answer.

Outside, there are no stars. Katie doesn't have to look out the window to confirm this. It rained all day. It's rained all day everyday since Katie got to Oregon four days ago—not the good kind of rain either, not the pounding, purifying, consuming kind of rain. This is more of an insistent drizzle. Her impressions of the state so far involve perpetual dampness, a sky the color of concrete, and nights that glow an eerie yellow from the city light trapped in heavy atmosphere. There are no stars.

Katie does not want to talk to Darryl. She does not want to listen to his message. She also does not want to listen to the fucking, both the parts she can hear for real and the parts she is more and more sure she is imagining. She does not want to imagine the fucking. She gathers her room key, a credit card, and her cell phone into the front pocket of her sweatshirt and leaves her room.

This isn't the first night Darryl has called. He also called last night, and the night before that, sounding worried. Darryl is not Katie's boyfriend. He is also not Katie's father or her brother or her boss or her landlord. He inhabits none of the male roles Katie would normally accept worry from. Of course, Katie doesn't have a brother or a boss. She had a boyfriend, but not anymore. Her father does not know she's left Reno and therefore has no reason to worry. She and her landlord are not particularly close. So, if someone is going to be worried, why not Darryl?

In the lobby, nobody is fucking. There is free coffee and some floral print couches, but Katie doesn't feel like sitting alone on a floral print couch and drinking crummy coffee. The lobby is attached to a diner by a double set of glass doors. Katie walks through one door and stands in the tiny vestibule between the motel and the diner. For a moment, she pretends she is on the space shuttle, in the airlock. She breathes slow, like she would if she were in a space suit with the helmet on. She reaches through zero gravity for the second door. Inside the diner is nothing like the inside of the space shuttle. A teenage waiter asks her if she'd like to sit at the counter or a booth. Katie requests a booth.

Darryl is a retired civil engineer. He is sixty-five years old and has a long gray ponytail and large, callused hands. Darryl is the president of the Reno Amateur Astronomers Club—an organization in which Katie is a member. This relationship does not, in Katie's mind, necessitate Darryl's calling every night she is out of town to check on her. Except it's clear to Katie that Darryl thinks of himself as more than just the president of a club in which she is a member. Katie can't tell if the role Darryl is aiming for is that of father, or brother, or boyfriend. He has recently started being very nice to Katie. He invites her over to use his telescope on clear nights and often gives her small errands to do for the club. Katie admits to herself that she likes this extra attention.

The teenage waiter comes back and offers coffee. Katie accepts even though it is probably the exact same coffee she passed up in the lobby.

Katie decides her business in Portland is, in a way, a club errand. She's here to collect the rest of Alex's star maps—to rescue them. Everyone in the club loves Alex's maps and when there is a meeting addressing parts of the night's sky for which Katie does not have a corresponding Alex map, the mood in the room is decidedly dour. Katie is tired of dour meetings, so she is rescuing the missing maps. But when Darryl calls, he doesn't even ask about the maps. He asks about Katie.

On the kids' menu, Katie notices an item called the Spaceman Waffle. It is described as a Belgian waffle topped with vanilla ice cream and strawberry syrup. If Katie were a little kid in this diner with her parents, she would have begged them to let her get a Spaceman Waffle and they would have said "No."

When Katie met Alex, he was in the process of drawing maps of the entire sky as visible from the Northern Hemisphere at different times of the year. Each map was a masterpiece, intricately detailed with a swirling, multi-colored sky, white stars and yellow planets. The constellations were marked out with the barest of white lines, labeled in Alex's impeccable script. The maps were both gently surreal and very accurate. At the time, Alex was finishing up a Master's degree in visual art, but the maps weren't for school. Each one he finished while they were together, he gave to Katie. He claimed, for him, the beauty was in the process, not the product. Once he was done, he didn't enjoy the maps nearly so much as when he was working on them. So he gave them to her. Katie affixed these maps to the ceiling of her bedroom and only ever took them down when she went to meetings of the Reno Amateur Astronomers Club.

If she were in this diner with Alex, they would have ordered a Spaceman Waffle to share and laugh about and maybe joke-fight about who got to eat the last bite of ice cream.

The trouble is, Alex had started drawing star maps before he ever met Katie. He'd drawn them when he lived here, in Portland, with another girl and had given those first completed maps to that girl. This means Katie only has a half set. Katie and Alex broke up six weeks ago at which time he moved back home to Boston. This means Alex will never make any more maps for her. Katie thinks this is very unfair to both her and the club.

The Spaceman Waffle is the only space-themed item on the menu. In fact, it's the only themed item at all. Everything else has a perfectly ordinary name, like Bacon Cheeseburger or Short Stack of Pancakes. Katie finds this to be a bit of a let-down.

Katie loves anything and everything having to do with outer space. She loves stars and constellations and galaxies and black holes. She loves NASA and grainy pictures of the moon. She loves imagining what it would be like to be inside a space capsule, orbiting the Earth. When she was a little kid, she wanted to be an astronaut more than anything. But as an adult, this dream seems increasingly unrealistic, like wanting to be a dinosaur or a superhero. Of course, astronaut is an actual job that actual people do. But when Katie thinks of astronauts, she thinks of muscle-y men and women with perfect balance and perfect vision who look great in jumpsuits. These are not attributes Katie sees in herself.

That's why, instead, she goes to the Reno Amateur Astronomers Club and why she's majoring in physics at the University of Nevada, Reno—to have a better understanding of the way the universe works, to feel closer to the stars and the planets. Unfortunately, physics, it turns out, actually has very little to do with stars and planets. It's mostly just math. But that's okay. If nothing else, Katie is very good at math.

Katie had been dating Alex for several weeks when she confessed her love of outer space to him and he said, "Well, I've got something you should have then," which turned out to be the first star map he ever gave her. It was so beautiful, so perfect. She took it with her that week to her Reno Amateur Astronomers Club meeting and everyone in the club oooh'd and ahhh'd and asked to see another next time. So Alex gave her another for next time. And then another each time he finished one.

Alex once told Katie this former girlfriend in Portland had not been particularly interested in astronomy. Still, Katie imagines she must have known enough to affix the maps to her ceiling and to look up at them each night before she went to sleep.

So, that's what Katie has been doing in Portland for the last three days. She doesn't know the former girlfriend's address, or rather, she doesn't know it exactly. She knows the former girlfriend's name. And that she lives in the southeast part of the city. The phone book in the motel lobby lists addresses in this neighborhood for three people with the same name as the former girlfriend. Some online sleuthing has turned up two more. Each day, Katie sets out on foot through the Portland drizzle, city map in hand, looking for these addresses. When she finds one, she doesn't knock on the door. Instead she sneaks around the house, looking in windows. She looks at the ceilings in each room. She wants to be sure she's at the right place before she risks explaining her mission to anyone inside. So far though, she's visited four out of the five addresses and no luck.

She doesn't really have a plan for what she'll do if she sees Alex's maps on someone else's ceiling. She knows she should use the time she spends walking to come up with some sort of strategy, but as she wanders through the neighborhoods, all she can think about is what life was like for Alex when he lived here, in Portland, with the former girlfriend. She imagines Alex holding hands with the former girlfriend as they stroll through the rain together, not minding the weather at all. He'd have worn an absurdly bright raincoat, picked out for him by the former girlfriend, which would hang off his long, skinny torso, the hood up to protect his shaggy hair. She imagines Alex fucking the former girlfriend under her ceiling of maps. He would have done things with her that he never did with Katie—weird things, exciting things, and at all times of the day. Then they would lie on their backs and he'd tell her which maps were his favorites, and what he'd been thinking about as he drew each one, something he'd never done with Katie, even when she asked.

So yes, Katie agrees, Darryl has reason to be worried. This behavior is worrying. Katie knows wandering on foot through Southeast Portland, looking in strangers' windows, obsessing about Alex, skipping classes, spending her student loan money on gas and a motel room and crummy diner coffee is not wise or healthy. But Darryl doesn't know what Katie is doing. All he knows is that she is going to pick up more maps from a friend of Alex's in Portland. She is running an errand for the club. That's all. Based on that information, there is no need for a phone call each evening. Even if he were her father or brother or boyfriend, it wouldn't be necessary.

The other thing astronauts have to be good at, in addition to balance, vision, strength, and jumpsuit-wearing, is being alone. Katie often thinks about Michael Collins, the third member of Apollo 11, who stayed behind while Neil Armstrong and Buzz Aldrin explored the surface of the moon. As he orbited, Collins repeatedly lost radio contact with both Earth and the lunar module whenever he reached the backside of the moon. Katie imagines the only thing he was able to do during those times was look out the tiny windows of the spacecraft at all the beautiful stars and planets and hope that when he got back around to the other side, everything would still be all right. She believes there's something heroic about being able to withstand that sort of isolation and thinks it's unfair that Collins is by far the least famous of the Apollo 11 team.

The description of the Spaceman Waffle has Katie in the mood for something sweet. But she doesn't want to order a comically named plate off the kids' menu. When the teenage waiter comes back, she asks to see a dessert list. He nods and returns a moment later with a cart covered in various slices of cake and pie.

All the desserts on the cart look pretty much the same. Katie can't even tell which are pies and which are cakes, which are berry and which are chocolate. She points to a plate on the far left end of the cart and says she'll have one of those. "The Boston cream," the teenage waiter says. Just fucking perfect, Katie thinks. But she doesn't want to change her order. She nods and he leaves with the cart.

When people who aren't her closest friends ask Katie what happened between her and Alex, she usually tells them he went home to Boston—or rather, some crappy suburb of Boston—because he could not find a job in Reno after he finished his degree and so his only recourse was to move back across the country and live with his mom. She tells these friends she and Alex discussed the option of the long-distance relationship, but had together, mutually, dismissed it since Katie still has another year before she's done with school and Alex did not know if or when he'd be able to return to the west. When she tells these friends this, she almost believes it's really what happened—that she and Alex are still friends and still a little in love and it's just the distance and the money that keeps them apart. She acknowledges this is an impressive leap of imagination since she was obviously present for all the arguments and the uncomfortable silences and the desperate make-up fucking and then the additional arguments (because desperate fucking never really solves anything) that preceded Alex's departure.

The teenage waiter sets Katie's order in front of her and hands her a rolled up napkin with silverware inside. She thanks him. She tastes the pie. It's just fine.

Weirdly, Darryl is one of the few people Katie has confided in about her break-up. Not about the fucking, of course. But about the rest of it. One night, after a meeting of the Reno Amateur Astronomers Club, Darryl put one of his big, callused hands on her shoulder and said, "Katie, are you okay?" And then it all came pouring out of her, right there in the doorway of the grange hall where the club has its meetings. Darryl just listened and nodded and when she was done with her story, he'd asked for the first time if she'd like to come out to his house the next night and use his telescope.

When Alex gave Katie her first star map, she thought she'd finally found a kindred spirit: someone who loved space just as much as she did. But this turned out not to be the case. Not totally. Alex liked stars okay, but only because they were something he could draw maps of. Mostly, Alex liked maps. He never went with Katie to the Reno Amateur Astronomers Club. If there had been a Reno Amateur Cartographers Club, he would have gone to that, he said, but there wasn't. Katie tried very hard at the time not to be disappointed by this. She understood it was unreasonable for one person to expect to ever find another person who could be everything that first person wanted. When they were breaking up, Katie had reminded Alex of this universal relationship truth and he said, "But that's not really the issue here, is it?"

A man and a woman walk into the diner together and sit at the counter with their backs to Katie. Katie isn't sure why, but she is absolutely certain they are the people who were fucking in the room next to hers. They are young—around Katie's age. The woman is tall with short brown hair. The man is man-sized and wears a baseball cap. Although Katie cannot see their faces, she senses from them the kind of mutual contentment that can only come from fucking aggressively in a bed that is not your own in a city with which you are largely unfamiliar. She sees this in their shoulders. In their cheeks, still flush from their recent exertions. In the way they lean their elbows against the counter for support. In the way, after they both take their first sips of coffee, the woman puts her left hand on the man's knee without looking at him. Katie decides she sort of hates them.

It's not like Darryl's ever tried to touch Katie or do anything pervy with her. That's not the problem. He just calls her too much. He invites her over to use his telescope too much. He favors her too much during club meetings, asking her to help him spread out charts or plot coordinates. He's too nice to her. Katie thinks maybe if she had more friends like Darryl, Darryl wouldn't seem so odd. But the fact is, Darryl is actually the only person to whom Katie has told the truth about Alex. And Darryl is the only person who knows Katie is in Portland. If he did try to get pervy with her, that would make everything easier. Then she could just tell him to go fuck himself. Then she wouldn't have to think about how weird it is to be a twenty-two-year-old college student whose only real friend is an aging amateur astronomer with a ponytail. She wouldn't have to think about what this situation says about her as a person.

Katie decides she is done thinking about Darryl for the night. She will put him out of her mind entirely. And if he calls tomorrow, she will answer, even if the people in the room next door are fucking, and she will tell him she is fine and she has picked up the star maps and she is heading home the next day and will drive safe and stop frequently along the way to stretch and eat balanced meals. She will tell him this even if it is not true, she decides.

Katie knows other things about Alex's former girlfriend aside from just her name and her possible addresses. She knows she worked for a while (and maybe still does) at an art supply store, which is how she and Alex met. She knows she enjoys music, cross-country skiing, and cribbage. She knows she has curly brown hair that falls over her shoulders. She knows she likes to wear big sun hats in summer. Katie knows some of these things from looking at the former girlfriend's Facebook page. And also because she used to ask Alex about her sometimes. Actually, if she is being honest, she used to ask Alex about her more often than just sometimes. Once, they had been discussing the former girlfriend and Katie said, "You're still in love with her, I can tell." Alex shook his head. "No," he said. "But I'm starting to think *you're* in love with her. You can't ever seem to stop talking about her."

So maybe Katie had asked about her too often. But she couldn't help it. She wanted to know what Alex's life was like prior to being with her. Had he been different in some way? Had he been happier? Katie was convinced he was. After all, who could possibly be happier in weird little Reno with Katie than in super-cool Portland with a woman who wears sun hats? So yes, she asked a lot of questions.

In the background of the former girlfriend's Facebook profile picture (the one where she's wearing a big sun hat), there's a bright yellow, two story house. The house has white trim and a little garden in the front. It's very cute. Katie does not know if this is the former girlfriend's house, but she imagines it must be, cute as it is, like the former girlfriend herself. Katie has yet to see this house during her time in Portland, though she looks for it on every street, even when she is nowhere near one of the addresses she has for women with the former girlfriend's name.

Katie watches the teenage waiter lead a family—Mom, Dad, little boy—through the diner. He installs them in the booth behind hers. Before the parents even have a chance to sit, the little boy orders a Spaceman Waffle. Katie figures they must be locals who, bending to the whims of their small offspring, come to this crummy motel diner on a semi-regular basis. It seems like a bummer way to spend an evening—indeed, Katie herself is here and definitely having a bummer evening. But she can also see an upside in the parents' case. They take the little boy someplace he likes, feed him a ton of sugar, take him home and let him run around all crazy and sugar high until he falls asleep on the couch. Then Mom and Dad can have some time to themselves. They can have quiet and contented sex, knowing they are, at the very least, okay parents and that their son loves them.

Katie wonders how long it will be until the couple at the counter have a kid and whether they'll take him to crummy motel diners just to make him happy.

Sometimes Katie and Alex used to speculate about what their kids would be like, if they ever had kids together. Or, rather, Katie would speculate and Alex would agree with whatever she said. Katie thought their kids would be pale, nearsighted, and skinny as straws. They'd have his shaggy brown hair and her green eyes. They'd be good at both art and math.

The Spaceman Waffle comes with a tiny plastic space shuttle sticking out of the vanilla ice cream. Katie sees this when the teenage waiter delivers it to the little boy at the booth behind her. It's a nice touch, she thinks.

If Katie and Alex had a kid together, they would have let him eat Spaceman Waffles all the time. They would have covered his bedroom walls in glow-in-the-dark stars. They would never have forced him to play sports or join church youth groups or even take baths if he didn't want to. They would have been ridiculously permissive parents. The most fun parents ever, Katie thinks.

The couple at the counter will not be fun parents. Sure, they're having fun, with each other, now. But in a few years, they'll settle in to a steady routine of pragmatism and practicality. They will be responsible, boring, normal parents. Katie pities them a little for their dull future, which will no doubt take place in a suburban tract home amid Ikea furniture.

Behind her, the little boy is making airplane noises. "Eat your waffle before you play with your toy," she hears the mom say.

Katie gives up on her Boston cream pie. It isn't just fine after all. The custard is too sweet and the chocolate on top tastes waxy and sticks to her teeth. She puts down her fork. She scoots to the edge of the booth, leans her back against the wall and stretches her legs out on the seat. Now she can see everything—the front door, the couple at the counter, the little boy and his parents. The little boy has eaten all of his ice cream but neglected his waffle entirely. When he sees Katie looking at him, he pulls himself up to the back of the booth seat between them. He pushes his space shuttle across the top of the booth. Katie imagines she can hear its tiny plastic wheels squeak when he does this, even though she knows she can't. "This is called taxiing," the boy says. "It's what happens before take-off." Katie shakes her head. "Space shuttles don't taxi," she says. "They take off straight up." She points up with her finger. The little boy shrugs and keeps taxiing.

This makes Katie think about why she, as a child, decided she wanted to be an astronaut in the first place and how it had nothing to do with stars or math or telescopes.

When Katie was in preschool, her parents took her and her older sister to visit a state park that housed a Paiute archeological site. The park had a program where kids were given worksheets and instructions to visit various locations around the site and draw pictures on the worksheet of what they saw. Everyone who completed a worksheet received a toy pickaxe and a plastic badge that said "Junior Archeologist." Katie filled out hers with the help of her mom.

On the car ride home, Katie could not remember her honorary title. She reached for the biggest word she knew that started with the letter "A." "When I grow up, I want to be a real astronaut," she announced. Her sister, already too big to be interested in plastic badges and toy pickaxes, was quick to correct her. "You mean 'archeologist,'" she said. "When you grow up, you want to be a real archeologist." And because even as a little kid Katie hated to be wrong, she said, "No, I mean astronaut" and held to the claim for so long it became true.

Maybe this was the reason she and Alex had broken up. Not because Katie wanted to be an astronaut, but because she hated to be wrong. Alex didn't mind being wrong. And so whenever one of them had to be wrong, it was always Alex. Maybe Alex just got tired of having to be wrong all the time.

Katie waves down the teenage waiter and asks him for a pen. He digs around in the pockets of his apron and hands her a blue Bic with a chewed up cap. She thanks him. On a napkin, she writes, "Things Alex Was Always Wrong About." Under this heading, she adds, "1) the importance of astronomy 2) the importance of agreeing on how to raise hypothetical children 3) the importance of making his current girlfriend feel like she's more important than his ex-girlfriend."

She wonders if Alex, at one point, made a list called "Things Katie is Always Wrong About," since he was actually the one who broke up with her. She wonders if at the top of this list was "1) the necessity of pestering her boyfriend about the importance of various things." She wonders now if Alex found this behavior, this constant questioning and speculating and comparing and pushing and doubting, to be oppressive. If he ever said so, she can't remember.

The little boy wants Katie's attention again.

"Like this?" he asks. He's got the toy space shuttle pointing straight up this time with its nose in the air.

"No, it's okay if you want to taxi first," Katie says. "You do it your own way."

The little boy shakes his head.

"Will you count down to blast off?" he asks.

Katie says she will. She starts with ten and then says nine and then eight and all the way down to one and then she says, "Blast off."

The little boy purses his lips then opens his mouth wide to make his rocket firing noise. It sounds like "Pow." He lifts the toy up as high as his arm will reach. He stands up on the booth seat to reach higher.

It's hard for Katie not to feel a little hopeless about her prospects of finding the maps. After four days in Portland, she is no closer to locating the former girlfriend than she was when she first arrived. And it is also possible Katie has erred in her belief that the former girlfriend values the maps as much as Katie herself does. It may be wrong to assume that she even still has them. Now, the more Katie thinks about it, the more convinced she becomes that the former girlfriend has not actually kept the maps at all. She has not hung them on her ceiling and does not look at them when she lies in bed each night. More likely, she destroyed them as soon as she and Alex broke up. Or gave them to a friend. Or dropped them off at Goodwill.

After all, why would this woman want some relic of her broken relationship literally hanging over her head? Katie thinks the former girlfriend probably made the right choice by purging Alex from her life entirely. Good for her. Like Michael Collins, the former girlfriend has found beauty, and maybe even solace, in her time spent alone. There is part of Katie that wishes she could do the same. After all, what good is it being hung up on someone who doesn't even care all that much about stars or what his future children might look like or if he always made Katie feel somehow less important than the woman who had been in her place before her?

Still, Katie knows tomorrow she'll go out in the rain again, looking for the last address on her list, scanning each street for the adorable bright yellow house with its adorable front yard garden.

"Now it's your turn," the little boy says, handing Katie the toy.

His mother interjects. "Ryan, that's enough. Let's let the nice lady finish her dessert."

"It's all right, I don't mind," Katie says, accepting the toy.

She sets the space shuttle on the back of the booth bench, pointing up, just like the little boy did. He counts down. He says each number slowly and deliberately. This is a little boy who takes his countdowns seriously.

When he gets to "blast off," she says "Pow," and lifts the space shuttle up, about half an arm's length, then flies it toward the little boy, landing it in his outstretched hand. He shakes his head. "That wasn't a very good blast off," he says. "You should do it again."

Katie looks to the parents to see if they've heard their small son's indictment of her blast off abilities, but they are absorbed in their own conversation, their bodies pressed close on their side of the booth. The father, smiling, whispers into the mother's ear. The mother laughs and whispers back. Katie imagines their exchange, something private and crude.

Across the room, the couple at the counter has adopted a similar posture. They lean, shoulder to shoulder, talking in low voices. Katie decides they are probably recounting their earlier fucking session. It was no doubt the greatest fuck of their lives thus far, and so they've got to keep replaying it over and over for one another right there at the counter.

Once again Katie stands the toy space shuttle upright and waits while the little boy does his deliberate and precise countdown. This time, when he gets to "blast off," Katie says "pow" like she means it, like it's an actual explosion. It's an extended "pow," guttural and drawn out, because space shuttles aren't launched by just one quick burst, but by rockets that continue to fire all the way up out of Earth's oppressive atmosphere. She lifts the space shuttle into the air. When she can't reach her arm any higher, Katie stands on her booth seat just like the little boy. She has to stop her explosion noise for a second to breathe, but when she starts again, it's with renewed energy and louder than before. She reaches the toy toward the diner ceiling. She stands on her tiptoes, hand and toy as far up as they can possibly go. The little boy smiles and claps. His parents stop their flirting to watch. The couple at the counter turn and look at Katie like they can't believe the ruckus she's making.

SPUD

SPUD II

May 21, 2077, Outer Space
Lieutenant Colonel Parker Timothy Olstead

It's been seven hours since the space shuttle Krona Ark III's electrical system ceased functioning. It runs now on its backup fuel cell, which powers only the barest of necessities: the oxygen generator, the pressurization system, and a thin rail of lights across the interior walls. He doesn't know how long the fuel cell is capable of sustaining them. Or how long they can last on their own, if it too fails.

He is frightened now and tries to think again of the ocean and the exhilarating notion that they are really just a ship lost at sea. A new kind of ship on a new kind of sea. What might Captain Cook have said in such a situation? Surely, he would not have abandoned hope.

But he is no Captain Cook. Therein lies the trouble with his analogy.

His Swedish shuttlemates move around him in a rush, floating from cabin to cabin, console to console, whispering foreign words to one another. They assure him they know what the problem is and are very close to fixing it. He does not question them. It's their shuttle and he is only a privileged guest. Besides, he's not an engineer. He's a marine biologist. He's here to learn how his squid and their protective bacteria react to unexpected modifications in their physical environment. From this data, he'll speculate how similar creatures on Earth will react to similar disruptions. Not that he anticipates Earth is about to experience a dramatic shift in its gravitational strength. But the planet is changing in marked and upsetting ways. The only way to predict the impact of one change is to observe other kinds of change.

That's the extent of his mission. And now, in the light of the current situation aboard the shuttle, it seems minor, even petty. He hasn't flown aircraft of any kind since his Air Force days, and even then his knowledge of the planes' inner-workings was theoretical at best. As for the Krona Ark III, here in its time of need, he is only a concerned passenger. All he can do is wish it well and nod encouragingly each time Edvard and Annika tell him they have everything under control. He wants to believe them.

"Do not worry," they say. "We have trained for this."

They call him Lieutenant Colonel when they speak to him. He hadn't noticed this before. They, like him, have been keeping their professional distance. But now he wishes they would call him by his first name. Parker. He wishes they would call him by his nickname. Spud.

He's been thinking about what to call the baby. He gets to choose the name. At first he wanted to name him after a personal hero—someone from the space program or the sciences. Michael Collins Olstead. Charles Darwin Olstead (who, himself, spent a good deal of time at sea). But those handles seem too weighty, too contrived. Shortly before boarding the Krona Ark III the previous morning, in a moment of familial affection, Olstead decided on a different name. He wants to name the boy for his mother, Samantha, ten years deceased, and also for his spinster sister, Caroline, who lives in their childhood home, barely eking out a living in Western Washington. Sam Carroll Olstead.

After all, family's the reason he agreed to take part in the clone program in the first place. He wants a family of his own. His mother is dead, his father ran off shortly after he was born, and his sister is so very different from him that, on the rare occasions they do see each other, he hardly knows what to say. As if they are strangers. In fact, that's how he feels in the company of most people, if he's being honest: estranged, and often alone. Easier to be around plants, animals, and fish.

But this little boy, he'll be just like him, exactly like him. It's impossible to feel alone when you've got someone else in the world who's exactly like you. It's a selfish desire, he knows. But he thinks, in a way, it will be good for his relationship with his sister, too. The arrival of a new generation always brings the previous generation closer. He'll take the boy with him whenever he visits her (he assumed this will be allowed, though he hasn't checked with the lab's director about travel policy). The boy will give them common ground, something to talk about, something to love together. The boy will share her name, and she can share with him an interest in the boy.

Now, though, he wishes he'd sent a note to the lab's director prior to the launch, detailing this name choice. Who knows what they'll call the boy otherwise.

Habitat

On summer evenings, the neon green hills of the Palouse sparkle and shimmer as if the Greenspree were waving back and forth in a gentle wind, catching the last of the day's light. It's a bucolic, almost surreal vision for passing drivers who don't know what they're looking at, who don't know that the shimmer and sway is actually the motion of thousands of snakes winding through acre after acre of an invasive fern that just happens to be the exact same color as their bodies.

This is the scene from almost every window in my dad's house as my brother and I work to remove light fixtures, built-in cabinets, light switch faceplates, anything, really, that can be stripped from the already empty rooms.

"The snakes are out," I say. We're upstairs in the master bedroom.

"What?" Kenton is inside the closet, pulling out shelves.

"The snakes are out," I say again.

"They've been out for an hour. You just weren't paying attention."

"No way."

"Maggie, they were out when we got here."

I tell him this cannot be the case. If the snakes had been out when we arrived, I would have insisted he turn the car around.

Half inside the closet, Kenton shrugs.

"They can't hurt you," he says.

"That's not the point."

I don't like the snakes. Nobody does. Kenton is right though—they can't hurt. Or rather, they choose not to hurt. They're skittish creatures, quick to dart out of sight as soon as something larger than them approaches. Mostly, they stick to the cover of the ferns where it's safe. It's rare to see even one out on the road, or really anywhere that isn't totally taken over by Greenspree. Which is good, because even by snake standards, they are ugly as sin.

They're called cob snakes and can grow up to twenty-four inches long, with narrow, tube-like bodies. Their eyes appear puckered, half closed, and they have skinny-long fangs that Kenton insists look like all other snakes' fangs, but I say worse—skinnier and longer somehow. And, with the exception of a single black stripe down their backs, they are entirely bright green, florescent green, almost: an identical shade to the Greenspree, even though they don't come from the same place and therefore could not possibly have evolved together in such a way.

Kenton and I are out at our dad's house, taking apart all the things there are to take apart because this is what Dad has asked us to do.

"You kids," he said. That's what he calls us when we're together, even though we're thirty-four. "I'd like you kids to bring me some things from the house."

I told Dad since the house now belongs to the state of Washington, it's probably illegal for us to be on the property, much less removing chunks of it.

"It's trespassing," I said. "And also vandalism."

"Come on, Maggie," Kenton said. "They're just going to bulldoze the house eventually anyway. What do they care if we take the doorknobs?"

Again, my brother was right. He usually is. Kenton is eight minutes older than I am and, ever since we began to talk, he's won almost every argument. He's also funnier than me, more confident than me, more ambitious than me, and a better driver than me. He's my best friend and the person who infuriates me most.

About the house: When the Greenspree first spread through the wheat fields of the Palouse, the state started buying out farmers, offering them cash for land. I think initially they'd hoped to fight the Greenspree and then sell the land back, but when the plant proved too aggressive, too hardy, the buyouts became a good-faith gesture. *Thank you, dear farmer, for your years of service to the great state of Washington. Now go buy yourself a mid-range condo.* That's exactly what Dad did eighteen months ago. Now he lives in a two-bedroom townhouse in Spokane. Instead of looking out over rolling hills of wheat, his view on all sides is of other two-bedroom townhouses. Instead of getting up at five o'clock each morning to go to work in his own backyard, he walks to the library downtown three days a week to shelve books for minimum wage. To keep himself busy, he says.

Another thing about the house: It's where Kenton and I grew up. I think Kenton always secretly assumed he and his wife, Elsa, would take over Dad's business and raise their own family there. I don't know where I would live in this scenario of his, but I imagine somewhere nearby.

Anyway, it will likely be bulldozed. Many of the abandoned homes and barns on the Palouse have been already, if for no other reason than uninhabited structures are a hazard. The best the state can do now is clear everything out of the way, let the Greenspree do its thing, and hope it stays confined to the Palouse.

It doesn't take long for us to finish taking everything there is to take out of the bedroom. Then we move on to the upstairs bath. I stand on the toilet seat to unscrew the overhead light while Kenton works to remove the shower door.

"Seriously?" I ask. "That?"

"Why not?" He adds the door to a pile in the hallway that already includes strips of crown molding, faucet heads, the closet shelves, a variety of handles and latches, a radiator baseboard, and a segment of copper pipe. It's weird to see this stuff separate from the rooms it's always been in. But then, it was weird to see the rooms without furniture when Dad first moved out. Someday soon, it will be weird to see this property without the house on it at all.

This is our second trip. We did the kitchen, den, and the half bath on the first floor last Saturday. When we got back to Spokane, Dad told us not to bring anything inside, just to take it all to his storage unit at the east edge of the condo complex. Neither of us asked what he planned to do with it, or why he needed it now, after a year and half of living without it.

I linger in the entryway and watch as Kenton carries stuff from the pile out to his truck. It takes him four trips, but I refuse to help. I don't want to be outside if the snakes are out. It doesn't matter that they won't bite, aren't poisonous, and want nothing to do with us. I still find them deeply unnerving.

Ultimately, I suppose, we're lucky when it comes to the Greenspree. It's restricted itself to the wheat fields, preferring soil that's soft and nutrient-rich. That's why you never see it in people's yards or anywhere else. Were it less picky, it could have consumed land across the entire Inland Northwest. Then, the snakes would be everywhere.

There are four rooms left—the basement, a small office, and the bedrooms Kenton and I slept in as kids. I'm standing in the doorway to my room, picking at a peeling strip of paint when Kenton comes in from loading the truck.

"Should we do these rooms today?" I ask.

"No. The truck's almost full. Next weekend."

I stare for a moment into the space where I spent so much of my childhood. Unlike Kenton, I wasn't a popular kid. I read books and played with my stuffed animals and kept my door closed, pretending I had a secret life the men in my house knew nothing about. Or rather, a secret life they would eventually find out about and when they did find out, they would be shocked and proud and say things like, "That Maggie, we always knew she had it in her." The place of my wildest and most sincere daydreams.

Then, there were other times when my room felt like the center of the world. Dad and Kenton, sitting on the floor, indulging me in imaginary tea parties. When we got older, me reading aloud to my brother from magazines while he fixed my computer. Kenton leaning against the doorframe after coming home from a party, telling me all the gossip so I wouldn't be left out. The room is still pink—the color I asked Dad to paint it for my sixth birthday.

"I'll do your room if you do mine," I offer. "It'll be easier that way."

"Not now," Kenton says. "Next weekend."

And so, another Kenton victory. By ignoring my offer, he gets to be the cool sibling—the rational one, taking everything in stride. Which would be fine, except, then what does that make me?

People often think Greenspree is named for its color. It's not. The full name of the plant is the Corbin Greenspree Deciduous Fern, after Corbin Greenspree, the botanist who first identified it as an independent species and observed its properties. One such property is a deep and lengthy root system. The plant is most commonly found on river banks in the southern United States, embedded in soil that looks as if it could, at any moment, give itself up to the water, but doesn't. As Corbin Greenspree noted, the ferns' roots actually help hold loose soil together. This is how the Greenspree ended up in Eastern Washington. One particularly rainy spring, a group of neighboring farmers purchased Greenspree to plant along the parts of their property that ran beside the Palouse River, to prevent erosion. The plant thrived in the cooler climate in a way no one had predicted. It spread, unable to be stopped, and within just a few years had taken over the wheat fields, crippling one of the region's oldest industries. The irony of this was not lost on the farmers who originally imported the plant.

As for the cob snakes, their origin is less clear. They, too, are naturally found in warmer places—specifically low lying hills in Central America. One theory of how they came to the Palouse is that a single pair were imported illegally as pets and later set free, or escaped. These two were the Adam and Eve of Washington cob snakes, a lone couple begetting offspring who then rapidly begat more and more offspring.

The other theory is that the cob snakes were always here, but had somehow gone unnoticed until the Greenspree arrived.

Whatever their story, they love the ferns. They live in the ferns, sun themselves in patches of light that cut through the ferns, feed on the rodents that burrow beneath the ferns, lay eggs in the burrows, and then hibernate there in the winters. It's the ferns that give the snakes their safe haven and the snakes that give the ferns their distinctive look. On cool summer nights, the snakes grow restless, ready to move and hunt and writhe, sliding through the ferns en masse, a sea of green-black bodies, surveying all that is theirs.

I work as a copyeditor for Spokane's daily newspaper. One of my co-workers, Catherine, is also from the Palouse. When we were kids, she lived just a few miles from my family, but I never knew her. As she tells it, her parents were "religious nut-jobs" who chose to home-school their daughter to protect her from the sinful influence of public education. This, according to Catherine, was a wasted effort. Like most Palouse kids (Kenton and myself included), Catherine moved to Spokane as soon as she was old enough. In addition to working for the newspaper, she moonlights as a nude model for the art school and fronts a punk band called Indigo Christ Punch. Her parents, however, remain faithful as always. When the Greenspree first started to spread, they took it as a sign of the impending rapture and fled to a compound in New Mexico.

On the Monday after Kenton and I make our second salvaging trip out to Dad's house, Catherine comes into my cubicle, holding a copy of *National Geographic.*

"There's a big article on us in there," she says.

"Us?"

"The Palouse. About the Greenspree and everything."

She sets the magazine down in front of me, and flips to a page near the middle. There's a panorama of the rolling hills, the iconic red barns, and the neon ferns, which, coincidentally, are a height and color similar to wheat in the spring, before it's ready to be harvested. So you actually have to look close enough at the picture to pick out the weird shape of the Greenspree's leaves in order to tell anything's amiss.

"It talks about how species from one area can go crazy-out-of-control when they're transplanted to another area because of lack of predators or climate or whatever used to keep them in check not being there. This isn't the only place it's happened."

I nod. "It's nice to finally be getting some national attention."

"And then there's this," Catherine says, opening a centerfold pullout to reveal a full-length photo of a cob snake, almost actual size, surrounded by facts and figures about the species. I quickly push the centerfold closed with Catherine's hand inside.

"Jesus, Catherine. Could you not?"

She laughs and picks up the magazine. "Sorry," she says. "I always forget."

I've never liked snakes. It's not that I've ever had a bad experience with one—in fact, I'm not sure I've ever had any experience with one. But I have always disliked them. It's something about the way they move, the shape of their heads, their quickness and coldness. Even pictures of snakes evoke a visceral response. Like a shiver. I can't control it.

Had we been different sorts of kids, this is a phobia my brother might easily have exploited. But he didn't. In fact, Kenton has always made a special effort to protect me from things I find distasteful or unpleasant. He'll warn me when cookies have nuts in them, or when the road to his house is icy. In high school, he went through the "Reptiles" chapter in my biology book and put Post-it Notes over the snake pictures so I could study without ever having to look at them.

After Catherine leaves, I read the *National Geographic* article online (in text-only format so I don't have to see the images). It's mostly information I already know except, as Catherine mentioned, the part about how what's happening here has happened other places too. In Minnesota, a mysterious aquatic plant clogs lakes, making them uninhabitable to most native fish. In West Texas, Eurasian wild boars, originally brought to North America by Christopher Columbus, have become so prevalent they threaten to destroy entire species of trees and shrubs with their constant digging and foraging.

These stories are alarming, but in a way, they're also comforting. This isn't a new problem, and it isn't an isolated problem. Ecosystems around the world are constantly under siege. They shift and struggle and adapt and move on.

So it's important to remember that what's happening to the Palouse isn't a catastrophe, necessarily. Just a change. Things change on Earth all the time. Mountains get taller and canyons get deeper. Glaciers melt. A new species of fish is discovered, on average, once every twenty-two days. Honey bees are going extinct. So are polar bears. One New Year's Day, 200 blackbirds fell from the sky, dead, onto the street of a small town in Arkansas.

The only difference is, this time it's here, where I live, and the displaced creatures are people I know. My dad, for one.

Ironically, just as Dad's world is shrinking, Kenton's is expanding. After almost a decade of slow, steady growth, Kenton's one-man graphic design company has experienced a sudden boon, and he's acquired new accounts not just here in Spokane, but from around the Northwest. On top of that, his wife, Elsa, is five months pregnant. The afternoon Catherine shows me the *National Geographic* article, Kenton sends me a text: "Dinner at Dad's @ 6. I'll bring pizza." I go over straight after work. When Kenton arrives, he's carrying not only pizza and a salad, but also a plate of brownies coated in thick blue frosting.

"Elsa's having dinner with friends from her office. She told me to tell you guys 'hi' though," Kenton says.

"What are these?" Dad asks, pointing at the brownies.

"Elsa made them. We found out today the baby's a boy."

For a moment, we all just stare at the brownie plate. No one in our family is keen on sweets.

"At least take a bite of one," Kenton says, "so I can tell her you had some."

"A grandson, eh?" Dad says. "Well now."

I watch Dad's face and I can see he's thinking of what it will be like to have a little boy around and he's pleased with the image. But I can also see this image isn't set here in the condo. It's at the old house: the boy bounding up the front steps, playing rough with Kenton out back. I watch his face as the image fades when he remembers.

"Congratulations, Ken," he says.

We eat and I grill Kenton on possible names for the baby. Kenton admits they've got one picked out, but won't say what. He claims they're keeping it a secret.

"Because it's something embarrassing?" I ask.

"No. Because we like having some things that are just ours, for now."

Kenton and Elsa have been married three years, but it still surprises me sometimes that he can have secrets with someone who isn't me. I think back to my childhood daydream—that I would be the one with the secret life, the one to move beyond the world of my father and brother in ways they would not expect. And yet, it seems things have turned out exactly the opposite. Kenton and Dad have their private lives of which I am not a part and often do not understand, while my own life is, for them, an open book. This seems unfair.

Before we leave, Dad's got another request from the old house.

"The wood-burning stove in the basement," he says.

"Okay," Kenton says. "No problem."

"You kids don't mind doing this for me, do you?" Dad asks.

We shake our heads. "Happy to help," we say.

People who don't know our dad well are often surprised to learn he's only sixty-three. The man looks and acts much older. He's sort of shrinking in to himself, a skinny guy with stooped shoulders and knobby hands. He doesn't talk much, either because he's become hard of hearing or he's run out of things to say. Most days, he doesn't bother to shave or comb his hair. He was already like this before the Greenspree swallowed up his wheat fields, but on his old property, he was a curmudgeonly farmer—an archetype of sorts. Now, in his sparsely furnished condo with few friends and not much to occupy his time, he just seems withdrawn, resigned, and a little sad. "He's got that widower look," Catherine said the first time she met him.

He is a widower, of course. Just not a recent widower. Our mother died when Kenton and I were three years old. We agree that we don't remember her.

Dad dated occasionally over the years, but never remarried. When we were kids, he seemed so solid in his independence, like he's never even needed anyone else. I respected that, and I like to think I'm the same in that way.

Except, if I'm being honest, I know I'm not.

So this thing with the stuff from the old house—that seems like another old man tic. It's not hoarding, exactly. More like he's stocking up, squirreling it away for a time when something will happen and he'll have use for it all again, when the streets and condos of Spokane fall away and the whole county will just be empty space. We'll need farmers like him then and he'll need his old light bulbs and banister posts. Or maybe that's not it at all. Maybe he just can't stand the thought living apart from things he used to love. Still, I don't ask and neither does my brother.

After dinner, on the walk back to our cars, I grab Kenton by his shirtsleeve.

"I want you to admit this is hard for you," I say.

"What's hard for me?"

"Dismantling Dad's house. Dismantling our house."

Kenton shakes his head.

"Maggie, you and I aren't the same person. I understand how you feel. But it's not that big a deal. This is just Dad being Dad—it is what it is."

I refuse to believe this.

"I know you," I say. "I know how you are."

Again, Kenton shakes his head. "If it bothers you so much, you don't have to come with me next week. I can get the rest by myself."

This is why Kenton wins every argument. He side-steps things. He makes whatever we're arguing about into something else. But I want to keep arguing about this particular thing. I want him to give.

"I know you wanted that house," I say. "For you and Elsa and your kid. I know you were planning on living there and working the fields."

This time Kenton laughs. "No," he says. "You think I want to raise my son on a wheat farm? That's not the life I want for him. Besides, I have my own business. What do I need Dad's for? That was never the plan."

"Then what was the plan?"

"Elsa wants to move to Seattle. She thinks it's the next step for my company, to be in a real tech market instead of out here in some city no one's ever heard of. Plus, the schools are better. After the baby's born, we'll probably start looking."

I am surprised by this, both that I was so wrong, and that Kenton, again, could have kept this secret. I want to ask if Dad knows. I want to ask if, in Kenton's image of himself and Elsa and their boy in Seattle, I am somewhere nearby. But I don't. Instead, I say, "No, it's okay. I can come with you again on Saturday."

"Good," Kenton says. "I'll see you then."

That Friday, Catherine and I sit outside during lunch hour, eating sandwiches from the office's deli cart.

"Sorry about the giant snake picture the other day," Catherine says.

"It's okay. It's a stupid thing to freak out about anyway."

"I just wanted to fuck with you a little. Nobody else in your life ever fucks with you. I can tell."

She's right about this. Kenton teases, but always gently. Dad, never. The handful of other friends I have are, on the whole, very polite.

"Thanks, I guess?" I say.

"You're welcome."

"I've heard they have this problem in Canada, too," Catherine says. "In Manitoba. Only with a different kind of snake."

"Because of plants?"

"No. I think just because snakes like Manitoba."

I am reminded again of the fickleness of nature. Or maybe what I actually mean is the precision of it. The right conditions in the right place can make all the difference, like in California where Joshua Trees refuse to grow outside of a few hundred feet of their preferred elevation. But where they do grow, they're everywhere.

"When your parents moved, did they take a lot of stuff with them?" I ask.

"No, actually," Catherine says. "Their compound wouldn't let them bring furniture or decorations or anything because everyone is supposed to appear equal before the eyes of the Lord or whatever. All their cabin has is a bed and a table and chairs. They could bring their own cookware, but that's it. Mom says she's the only woman there with a fondue set, so she's pretty popular. Everything else, they mostly just gave away."

"How did you feel about that?"

"I got their couch and some bookshelves, so that was nice."

I ask her if she has been back to the house since then.

"Oh God no," she says. "As far as I'm concerned, the ferns and the snakes can have that place."

I know what Catherine has said is meant to be funny and so I laugh along with her. But I'm also tremendously jealous. I'd give anything to feel the same way.

On the drive out to the Palouse on Saturday I think about my offer to Kenton from the previous trip—that I'll strip the remnants from his old bedroom if he'll do mine. But I decide this arrangement won't make the job any easier. I don't want to dismantle what little is left of Kenton's childhood any more than I do my own. I am momentarily angry with Dad for asking this of us, as if he's the only one affected by the Greenspree and the cob snakes and the loss of the house. But, of course, then I remember that in the grand scheme of things, Dad's been hurt so much more by all our collective losses—like he's the family punching bag, absorbing the worst of the shocks before they can get to me and Kenton. So who am I to begrudge him the last pieces of his home, if that's his wish? Still though, I am ready to be finished with this project.

It's like Kenton's read my mind, because when we pull off the highway he says, "How about we just get the stove and be done with it?"

I agree to this plan.

"If Dad wanted anything else specifically, he would have said so," he adds. "Besides, it's not like he's got big plans for any of it."

"I think it's supposed to be our inheritance."

Kenton smiles at this. "I would have preferred cash."

"You aren't excited to pass the family light socket covers on to your son?"

"I'll let you keep those. I know how much you've always cared for them."

He's teasing of course. His kind of teasing—harmless and meant only to get a smile out of me when he knows I need it. This is what I'll lose if Kenton moves—a day-to-day connection with the one person who always understands. Or, if not always, at least ninety percent of the time.

We park in the gravel driveway. It's early in the day, too hot for the snakes to be active, and so the Greenspree is still. Down in the basement, though, the air is markedly cooler. There's a stale, musty smell I don't remember. I have no desire to linger here and it's clear neither does Kenton. He leaves the door open and keeps wiping his hands against the front of his jeans like he's just touched something gross.

In all likelihood, the stove hasn't ever been used. There's no chimney for it and it's in a weird spot, pressed against the wall next to a workbench. Kenton braces himself against the workbench and rocks the stove back and forth to move it from the place where its legs have sunk slightly into the unfinished dirt floor of the basement. Once he's done that, he gives the stove a push, moving it two or three feet toward the center of the room.

"Heavy," he says.

"Duh," I say.

The wall the stove was blocking has a fist-size hole in it—like maybe at one point a pipe or wiring emerged from there. Or maybe the hole was an accident of some sort. Either way, it seems entirely possible the stove's sole purpose has always been to cover it up.

Kenton taps at the edge of the hole with the toe of his boot. He bends down and peers inside. Then he straightens up and jumps back.

"Oh shit!" he says.

From the hole in the wall emerges a cob snake. It sticks its head straight out and tests the air with its tongue, then lowers itself, face first, to the floor. A second snake immediately follows.

I wonder if fear is always just a matter of degree—if, subconsciously, everyone is afraid of the same things. It's just a matter of how close we feel to those things at any given time that determines whether or not our fear manifests in a way we can detect.

Kenton puts an arm in front of me, steering me behind him. A protective gesture. I mean to remind him the snakes won't bite, but of course I'm scared, too, so I say nothing, just stand and watch them try to navigate the rutted basement floor.

"Shit," Kenton says again. "It could be a burrow."

I don't know if this can happen with cob snakes, but I've heard horror stories of other kinds of snakes getting into walls, taking over houses. We wait a moment longer, but no others come through the hole. These two are alone.

"How did they get in there?" I ask.

"How did any of them get anywhere?" he replies.

I can tell Kenton's initial surprise has worn off and he is no longer afraid. I'm also calmer than I would have expected. Weirdly, being in the same room with the cob snakes is less alarming than seeing pictures of them or looking at them in the Greenspree from a distance. They don't seem to notice us at all.

"I'll take them outside," Kenton says. "You can go wait upstairs."

The two snakes are probably mates, but that's not what I think of at first. My first instinct is to wonder if they are brother and sister, hatched from the same clutch of eggs and together everywhere since. I worry if Kenton returns them to the field one at a time, skittish as they are, the first will bolt as soon as it's released, with or without its twin. Then they will be separated and it might be hard for them to find one another again. I do not want this for them.

"No," I say. "I want to help."

I can see my brother is surprised by this offer.

"Okay," he says. "Go grab them. I'll hold the door for you."

"Don't tease. I might change my mind."

We look around for some sort of containers to corral the snakes into. Since we've spent the past three weekends emptying the house of everything that isn't (and in some cases, that is) nailed down, options are limited. Kenton runs out to the tool shed in the back and returns with a piece of firewood and a stack of those plastic pots nursery plants come in. I can't remember anyone ever planting flowers in our yard. I think about how they must have been in the shed since before our mom died.

"How do you want to do this?" Kenton asks.

The snakes still haven't gone very far from the hole. I wonder if they are disoriented, or if it's just a temperature thing—something about that specific patch of floor that's particularly pleasant.

I tell him to trap the first snake and give it to me and I'll hold it while he gets the second one. Then we can take them out to the Greenspree where they belong.

Kenton does this, cornering one against the wall and ushering it into the container using the firewood. He fits a second container against the top of the first and, with both hands, holds the whole arrangement out to me.

"All yours," he says.

Inside the container, my snake is freaked. It thumps against the thin wall of plastic that separates it from my hands. I imagine it squirming around, knocking its head as it flails, looking for any possible way to escape. I do not like this feeling. But I hold the container tight and wait while Kenton wrangles the second snake. After what feels like forever, he says, "Okay, let's go."

We walk up the basement steps, out the back door, across the yard that used to be grass, but is now just dirt and a few weeds.

Kenton's in the lead. He's got longer legs than me, moves faster. Two more ways my sibling has the advantage. He reaches the place where the yard meets the fields of Greenspree well before I do. He bends like he's going to set his container down. Too soon.

"Wait," I say.

Kenton straightens up and waits. My snake thrashes and shakes. I wonder what it will do when I let it out—if it will be angry or relieved, if it will follow Kenton's snake or go an entirely different direction. It occurs to me that releasing them together may not actually ensure their continued partnership.

Still, I tell Kenton I want us to open our containers at the same exact time, on the count of three, and he agrees.

SPUD

SPUD II

July 15, 2090, Bainbridge Island, Washington
Parker Timothy Olstead II

The dog follows them up the beach and down the trail to the cluster of low houses with sloped, mossy roofs. They stop at the second house from the street, Camden and Twila's, and Spud tells the dog to wait, even though he knows it will anyway. His aunt says he's "got a way with animals." He spends hours observing the creatures that live along the beach and in the woods. He tries to read them like he would a book. He knows their habits, and usually he can get them to do what he wants. Frogs will rest on his knees if he puts them there. Once, a heron ate breadcrumbs from his hand, its long neck stretched out to reach him. The dog is loyal and shows no interest in anyone else.

Inside, Camden leads him to the basement—ostensibly toward paperwork she's found relating in some way to his father. He only half way trusts such a thing really exists. Camden has always been a liar. Though it's only the last year her lies have turned mean. Or, if not mean, manipulative. Lies to control, lies to confuse.

There's part of him that wants this to be just another one of those lies. That way he won't really be breaking the promise he made to himself on the beach just an hour ago—no more pathetic pining for his dead and absent parents.

He's been in this basement before, but not for a long time. Not since he and Camden were small, back when they were real friends and used to play hide-and-seek while his aunt and Camden's mom clipped coupons in the kitchen and did whatever else. In the basement, there's a couch, a desk, three mismatched chairs and a file cabinet. Camden opens the bottom drawer of the cabinet and makes a big show of sifting through it. He wonders if she actually found the file somewhere else in the house and re-hid it here as a means to get him down to the basement, where, even if Twila does come home suddenly, they won't be interrupted. That would be just like Camden—always thinking one step ahead of him, getting him to do exactly what she wants, when she wants, where she wants.

After what seems like too long a time, Camden pulls a worn-looking manila envelope from the drawer and holds it up. The envelope is, as Camden promised, fat with papers. The edges are creased and torn in some places, exposing white pages within.

"See?" she says. "I told you."

"Lieutenant Colonel Olstead" is printed neatly across the top and a return address for the University of Michigan in the right corner. He grabs for the envelope and is surprised when Camden drops it into his hands without a struggle. Inside are pages with numbers: cholesterol, white blood cell count, height, weight, pulse. Spud feels his phone vibrate in his pocket. He ignores it. He knows it's his aunt because she's the only person who ever calls, and she only calls when she has some chore she wants him to do. He doesn't want to do her stupid chore today. As a man of thirteen years old, he shouldn't have to, he decides. He keeps flipping through pages, but none of them mean anything to him. A red stamp appears on the last sheet of paper. APPROVED.

"It's just medical stuff," he says.

"Does it look important?" Camden asks.

"Well, he's dead, so it can't be that important now."

"I mean does it tell you anything about him as a person, idiot."

"Tells me my dad once got a physical at the University of Michigan. So what?"

Camden reaches for him and he shifts to avoid her, but she only puts her hand across his. The touch surprises him—tenderness he's not used to from his neighbor. He feels hot tears welling up behind his eyes. He doesn't want to cry.

"I'm sorry, Spud," Camden says. "I was really just trying to help. I don't have a dad either and I know how much…" But he hardly hears her. He needs to get away from her. She's lured him into breaking his promise to himself and for what? The tiniest scraps of information. As if information would bring a person back to life. Stupid.

Worse still, the information she presented him with was useless. Whatever's in the file holds no value for him. And now, here's Camden, being nice to him, feeling sorry for him. How fragile must he seem if even Camden—conniving, catty, horny Camden—has to treat him with kid gloves? He doesn't want her pity. It's ten times worse than her baffling flirtations, or even her blatant cruelty.

He scrambles to his feet, pushing her hand away. He feels, suddenly overwhelmed in his loneliness, like a flood of water has washed over him. No, not a flood. The whole ocean. He is inside the middle of an ocean, vast and crushing pressure from the unending water surrounding him.

"I'm sorry, too," he mumbles.

Then he's up and out of the basement, out of the house fast and the dog is there, waiting. He bends over so he's down at dog-eye level. He considers pulling the dog in, holding it to his chest. He wants desperately to be close to someone. But not Camden, not his aunt, not any of his aunt's dull, cow-eyed friends. He wants someone, or something that understands him. Then he's mad for that, too. Mad that he's been put in a position where he has to convince himself that *dad* and *dog* are interchangeable. Fuck the interconnectedness of all things, he thinks. If it were true, he could not possibly feel so lonesome.

Really, he decides, the truth is the exact opposite. Nothing is connected and everyone is isolated, spinning quietly on their own private planets, victims of gravity and time. Any illusions of shared experience are just that—illusions. And on the rare occasion people in their sad, private planet bubbles do interact, it only leads to pain.

This idea comes as a relief.

Pain is better than loneliness, he decides. After all, he can choose to feel pain, and he can choose to inflict pain. This is a power he possesses. This is a power he, today, as a man, can exercise.

So, he doesn't hug the dog. Instead, he slaps it in the face as hard as he can. For an instant, the dog just looks at him. Then it does what Spud knows any animal full of teeth and muscle should. It lunges.

Excitable Creatures

The animal sitting in the middle of your backyard is not a dog. It is also not a pig, or a bear. It has a wide, muscle-y body, a pushed up nose, and big, sympathetic eyes. It looks at you like it wants something from you. You go back inside and cut up chunks of cheddar cheese, which you offer to the animal, first on the ground, then from your hand. The animal is wary, but after a few moments grows comfortable with the idea of eating from your palm and even licks the last crumbs of cheese off your fingers when it's done. You tentatively scratch at the top of its bulky head, which it allows. This is the most satisfying interaction you will have with another living being all day.

Your yard has no fence. A row of trees separates you from your neighbor on one side and a shallow creek marks the boundary between your property and the woods. A subdivision of prefab houses has recently gone in across the street, much to your chagrin, but here in your yard, it's still easy enough to pretend that you are alone—the sole homesteader carving out her niche in the rugged western wilderness. Or something like that. It is reasonable to assume the animal simply wandered over from the neighbors' house. Or out of the woods if it's wild. But the way it looks at you as it sniffs the ground for cheese remnants makes you think its arrival is somehow more deliberate. As if it was put there just for you. This day, in particular, you feel you deserve something special.

This day is a Wednesday and it is also your third-to-last day at work. This is not your choice. You're being laid off. Or you're being fired. Or you're being let go. You're unclear about the distinction between these phrases and it hardly matters anyway. Today you will go to work and answer phones. Tomorrow you will go to work and answer phones. Friday you will go to work and clean out your desk and say "Thank you" when someone hands you a goodbye card everyone else in the office has signed and you will promise to keep in touch with this person, and maybe even accept a hug from him or her, even though you do not actually like him or her. On Monday, you don't know what you will do. Probably start looking for another job answering phones.

You decide to leave the animal alone and if it's still in your yard when you get home, you'll do something about it. You aren't sure what.

The company that has employed you for the last four years—and the next three days—manufactures small plastic parts for other companies that make electronics. Your job is to take orders for these small plastic parts and then to let the customers know when their orders have been filled and shipped. Although no one has said as much to you explicitly, you suspect there are computer programs that could do your job. This is likely why you are being laid off/let go/fired.

At work, you act like it's any other day, even though it's your third-to-last day. You answer the phones and you place calls. When Gretchen, your supervisor, asks how your morning is going, you say, "Good, thanks" and ask her the same question in return. She tells you about how her son scored a goal in soccer last night and when it's clearly your turn to volunteer some piece of personal (but not too personal) information in the name of continuing small talk, you're tempted to discuss the animal, which you found in your yard, and the way its tongue felt, warm and a little scratchy when it licked cheese bits from your fingers, but instead you talk about the movie you're planning to see on Saturday. Neither of you mentions your termination.

If you had to say what's the worst part about losing your job, it wouldn't be anything to do with the job itself. You've never had any real passion for the position, or affection for your co-workers, and so you won't miss either of those things. Money, of course, is a bigger concern, but you'll get a severance and then you'll get another job and then things will be the same as always. The sting comes from the knowledge that at your age, which is no longer a young age, you are still so totally and completely dispensable. You have carved out no niche of your own, staked claim to no territory, professionally. You possess no skills, or abilities, or insights to separate you from the rest of the herd. You regret this, but are unsure what decisions you could have made differently.

Back home, you sense the animal before you see it. You change out of your work clothes, pour yourself a glass of wine, and go out to the back porch. The animal is curled up in the grass, just where you first found it, asleep. You watch it for a minute. Its broad shoulders rise and fall with each breath, the fur on its back a thick black ridge. This is a powerful animal. But also, a cute animal. Its ears are little points, almost dainty. Its face has a softness to it, a nurturing quality. You clear your throat in hopes of waking it without startling it. It doesn't stir. "Excuse me," you say, first at normal volume, then a second time, louder. The animal opens its eyes and looks at you. Then it yawns. Is there anything cuter than a yawning mammal? You don't think there is. "All right," you say, "you just wait right there." Back inside, you fill a plastic salad bowl with leftovers—chicken, brown rice, and some vegetables—and take it out to the animal. "This is for you, in case you're hungry," you say. You think about how you should feel foolish talking to the animal like that, like it's a person who can understand and respond, but actually you feel totally normal.

You make dinner for yourself, watch the news, and go to bed early. Before you do, you look into the backyard and through the darkness you can see the animal: a speed bump sized protrusion in your grass. You're glad for this. You take pride in the fact that such an animal might deem your yard a worthy place to spend the night.

Thursday morning, the animal is still there. And when you get home from your second-to-last day of work the animal is also still there. What it's done while you were gone, you have no idea. There are no signs of digging or chewing in the yard. You assume it mostly slept.

This time when you walk outside with a bowl of food (deli ham, corn flakes, apple slices), the animal stands and shuffles over to you, its hindquarters wiggling as if it were trying to wag the tail it doesn't have. You can't help but smile at this. You watch as the animal eats—quickly, with its whole head jammed in the salad bowl. When it's done, you turn on the hose and let it drink from the spout. Holding the hose with one hand, you reach down with the other and run your fingers across the animal's back. The fur is so coarse, it's almost spiny. You move to its head next. You find a patch of soft fur behind its ears and you linger there, scratching at the spot. "Does that feel good?" you ask the animal. It snorts, spraying water from the hose onto your legs. You interpret this as a "yes."

You should be making plans. You should be hunting through classified pages and updating your résumé. You settle down in a chaise lounge on the back deck with a notepad. "Viable Career Options" you write at the top. But nothing comes to you and so you draw a sketch of the animal instead and when you are pleased with your work you stick the page on the refrigerator door with a magnet.

On Friday, you wake up early. You shower, get dressed, and pack a lunch just like it was any other day even though you don't plan on staying at work for more than an hour and certainly not until noon. You've got your keys in your hand and are about to walk out the door but you turn and walk back into the kitchen instead. There's something so miserably pathetic about this—going to work and having to pretend it's all fine and normal, surrounded by people for who the day is just a normal day and who won't really notice much at all when you are gone. You don't want to feel this pathetic. You decide you ought to have some company.

You grab the block of cheese from the fridge and rip off little pieces, using them to lure the animal from the backyard along the side of the house to the driveway. You open your car door and put two chunks of cheese on the backseat. The animal sniffs the air for a moment, as if weighing its options, then hops, more gracefully than you'd have expected, into the car. It takes up most of the back seat and has no interest in sticking its face out the window. It lies with its head on its paws for the entirety of the ride.

Inside the office, just holding the cheese is enough keep the animal at your side. You direct it into the elevator, down the hallway, past the girl at the front desk. Her face betrays visible alarm, but she makes no move to stop you. The animal follows you all the way through your office door and, with just a little bit of prompting, into an out-of-the-way space between two filing cabinets. It lies there, seemingly content, while you make your last phone calls. There aren't many calls to make, really. The computer programs have probably already taken over most of your tasks. You're done in forty-five minutes. You've brought a milk crate with you and start loading your few possessions from your desk. Gretchen enters your office while you're doing this.

"Heya, how's it going?" She's talking to you, but looking at the animal. The front desk girl must have tipped her off. You only shrug in response, not wanting to encourage small talk. You wish she would leave so you could finish your packing and be through with this place.

"Just so you know, we're not supposed to bring pets in the office," she says. "Unless maybe if they're service animals. Is that a service animal?"

You tell her no, it's not a service animal.

"Then I'm pretty sure it's not allowed," she says.

You tell her you hardly think it matters now.

She looks to the door, clearly hoping for someone else to appear with whom she can confer about the animal issue. Then she looks back to you.

"Is it a dog?" she asks.

You shake your head. She leans over, hands on her knees, as if she has suddenly decided the animal requires very careful scrutiny. You find you no longer want her to leave. You enjoy having this power over her—the power of owning something she can't identify. Though to be fair, you have yet to identify it either.

"Is it a wombat?" Gretchen asks.

"No," you say. "I think those only live in Australia."

"It looks like a wombat."

You shrug and reach down to scratch the soft place behind the animal's ear. It responds with a satisfied grunt.

"He likes it," Gretchen says, her voice softening.

"You can try if you want," you offer.

Gretchen looks to you, then back to the animal.

"No," she says. "No, that's all right."

She straightens up, brushing her hands against the front of her skirt, as if she's just discovered it covered in something unpleasant.

"Well…" she says.

"Well," you say.

"You keep in touch now," she says. "Don't be a stranger, you hear?"

"I'll have Steve from security come help you with your boxes," she adds. Then she leaves.

When Steve from security arrives, he makes no mention of the animal, just walks around it as if it were a piece of furniture. You, in turn, pay as little attention as possible to Steve from security.

At home, you find the animal follows you out of the car and up the driveway without the aid of cheese. You open the front door and stand to the side, hand outstretched. "I suppose you can come in if you want," you say to the animal. It accepts this offer with neither enthusiasm nor trepidation. It simply shuffles inside as if it's been crossing your threshold every afternoon for years. It pads across your hardwood floors to the rug in front of your TV, sniffs, turns around once and lies down. This is its spot. This is where it belongs.

This is also where you belong. You've lived in this modest house at the edge of town for most of your adult life. You own it outright and it's one of the few possessions you take real pride in. You like the open yard, the woods that run behind the house and to one side, the quiet and stillness of the place—an oasis just for you. Even with the new subdivision across the road, the land around your house still feels untamed, the way the woods creep right up to the edge of the street, like you or your neighbors could just fall into them and never be seen or heard from again.

You decide the time has come to give the animal a name. You first consider names that make reference to its bulk, like Mungo, Thor, Tank, or, in the more ironic vein, Tiny, Slim, or Mouse. Ultimately, you settle on Walter, after your grandfather. This is actually the name you had been planning on giving your son, were you to have a son, but it seems you have reached a point in your life where the son-having boat has pretty much sailed. So no sense hanging on to a perfectly good name.

Although you've bestowed the animal with a boy's name, you're not one hundred percent certain it's actually male. It never rolls onto its back (preferring instead to sleep on its stomach with arms and legs splayed out), or offers any other way for you to easily check. You don't want to press the issue. So you simply assume the animal is a boy because you like saying "Good boy." Much more satisfying than the alliterative, yet halting "Good girl."

Once you've given Walter his name, you feel he ought to have other things a pet might have as well. At a strip-mall pet store, you browse for a while before settling on a retractable leash and collar set that says XL on its tag and claims to be suitable for dogs up to 120 pounds. You suspect Walter may weigh more than this, but it will have to do. You also pick out a bag of rawhide chew sticks and a big orange rubber ball that squeaks when squeezed.

You don't know if Walter will be interested in playing fetch with you, but you figure it can't hurt to try.

The teenage girl working the cash register fondles your oversized purchases and smiles.

"What kind of dog do you have?" she asks.

"A Saint Bernard," you say, although if Walter were a dog, which you remain certain he is not, he would be closer to a Labrador. A Labrador mixed with a porcupine and a bison.

"Oooooooooh!" the girl squeals. "Those are my favorite! They're so cuddly. What's its name?"

"Walter," you say.

"That's a good name for a dog. I hope he likes his new toys," she says, handing you your bags.

You nod and smile back at her, satisfied in your abilities as a namer and caretaker of large creatures.

Outside the store, you stop to look at a bulletin board covered with fliers for free puppies, dog walkers, and animal training services. You notice also a number of posters for missing pets: cats and one small dog. The addresses are mostly from the subdivision across the road from you. Sad, you think. But this is what happens when people crowd themselves in to previously unpeopled places. The wild and the domesticated clash.

Walter, as it turns out, has no interest in fetch. Back home, in the yard, you wave the toy in front of his face and squeak the squeaker. He doesn't respond. You throw the toy across the yard. He watches it bounce twice and come to rest under some bushes, but makes no move to retrieve it. You don't take this personally.

His reaction to your other purchases is more favorable. You fit the collar around his bulky neck and when you attach the leash and tug gently, he stands and allows himself to be led in slow circles around the yard. Every few steps, you offer a reassuring "Good boy." He matches your stride and doesn't pull or stop abruptly. From then on, you lead him on walks through the woods behind your house each day. During these walks, you think about how you should be looking for work, how it is wrong to spend your days so free and unoccupied and unproductive. You watch as Walter sniffs and grunts with interest at his surroundings, and take pleasure in his company. You try to think of something, career-wise, that you might enjoy just as much and come up empty. The world of human work holds little appeal for you. You decide the problem is that you are perhaps more animal at heart.

The woman who comes to your door one afternoon looks concerned. She holds her hands behind her back and you can tell she is trying to sound casual. She is sharply dressed in heels, pleated slacks, a snug-fitting sweater, and her hair pulled back in a high ponytail. She doesn't look religious so you assume she has come to ask if you are registered to vote. But when she gets past her pleasantries, you see it's something else entirely.

"I live down the street," she says, pointing to the subdivision. "I'm going around the neighborhood to let people know about an issue that's come up."

She waits for you to nod and when you do she continues.

"My family and several other families have lost cats in recent weeks. We're worried there's something in the area that's hunting around here. Coyotes, maybe. So we're going door-to-door to warn other pet owners to keep their animals in at night. Do you have pets?"

"Yes," you say.

You see the woman look past you, scanning your living room. You tell her you appreciate the information and are sorry for her loss. You ask what her cat looks like.

"Sometimes they just wander off into the woods," you say, gesturing toward your yard, "and then turn up a few days later. I'll keep an eye out for it."

The cat is gray, the woman says. "But I doubt…"

Something has caught her attention. Behind you, you can feel Walter moving around. The woman's eyes grow wide.

"Is your dog part wolf?" she asks. "Yes," you say because it is no less correct than it would be to say "no." "I'll keep an eye out for your cat," you say again. The woman nods, thanks you quickly but politely, turns, and then is gone, back down your porch steps and across the street, back to her own side.

You'd be lying if you said you hadn't considered the possibility that Walter is responsible for the disappearing pets. When you're at home, he's inside with you or out in the yard. But you don't know what he does while you're gone. You leave the back door open so he can go out when he likes. You simply choose to assume, since he is always on your property when you return, that he stays there. But this may not be the case. This is likely not the case.

"Walter," you say, your hands on your hips in angry-housewife-position, "did you eat that nice woman's cat?"

Hearing his name, Walter looks up at you. You know he hasn't understood your question. Obviously. Still, there's something in his eyes, or in the way he cocks his head, that suggests comprehension. You smile in spite of yourself and are immediately ashamed. If Walter is guilty here, then you, as his owner, must also be. You do not want to be complicit in the death of cats. But there is a feeling of shared conspiracy you find satisfying.

That night you have a dream where you and Walter are hunters. Together, you roam the neighborhood, looking for prey. Except, there is no neighborhood. The subdivision is gone and your house stands alone at the end of the road, the way it did when you first moved in. But the people are still there. All through the woods, women wearing heels, pleated slacks, and snug-fitting sweaters, their hair pulled back in high ponytails—just like the woman who came to your door—walk with great purpose. They are unloading groceries from sport utility vehicles, getting their children ready for school, ironing more snug-fitting sweaters. Even without their homes, they look smug and content, bolstered by their sense of rightness in doing and owning the same things as everyone else around them. They take no notice of you. In the dream, you become disoriented in the maze of suburban women among the trees. You've lost sight of Walter, but somewhere in the distance you hear him howl—a high, tinny sound the real Walter never makes. You follow the sound and find him digging frantically at a hillside burrow. You pull him back by his collar and reach for whatever he's after. It's a mammal of some sort—not quite a cat, not quite a rodent—and when you pick it up, it is soft like a cotton ball and weighs almost nothing. "Walter, we can't eat this," you say, but then Walter howls again and you feel your hands close around the small creature, crushing it.

You wake with a sense of unease.

You sit out on the deck in the morning light with your notepad and start another list. This one is called "Ways to Make Sure Walter Stays in the Yard." You don't come up with anything. You sketch the cotton ball animal from your dream. In your drawing it is alert and fluffy and not crushed. You add this sketch to the fridge with the other.

The next day, you see Gretchen in the grocery store and although she looks straight at you, she doesn't acknowledge you. You've never liked Gretchen, but still, this deliberate avoidance irritates you. If the roles were reversed, you would at least be civil. You would at least wave and mouth "hello." You wonder, as you shop, what it would take to force Gretchen's attention. Some sort of public scene? If you had Walter with you, she wouldn't have been able to pretend she couldn't see you. She would have stared, just like your last day at the office.

You're aware you could simply go up to her and say "hi," and of course she would respond, even pretend to be happy to see you. But, again, you don't like Gretchen. So why bother?

Back home, you feel anxious, jittery. You try to convince yourself you aren't upset about Gretchen, but it's a lie. You decide you need to take a walk and clear your head. You find Walter asleep in his usual spot in the living room. You attach the leash to his collar and gently pull.

"Let's go," you say, and Walter stands and follows.

This time though, instead of going through the backyard, you lead Walter out the front door and across the street. Here, you can walk into the woods to the left or you can zigzag into the subdivision and meander among the prefab houses, manicured lawns, identical green mailboxes. You pick the subdivision.

Even with all this new stimuli, Walter is content on his leash, as always. He walks by your side and sniffs at things as you pass—trees, shrubs, children's toys left out in yards. He doesn't pull. "Good boy," you tell him from time to time. "Walter's a good boy."

The subdivision is nothing like in your dream. You knew this, of course. You've been here before, many times. Still, some part of you expects to see the identical women in their pleaded slacks and high ponytails walking with purpose to and from their identical SUVs parked in each and every driveway, their eyes clear, their expressions self-satisfied. Instead, the neighborhood seems all but abandoned. There are few cars on the street and most homes have their shades drawn. This makes sense—it's early afternoon on a weekday. Most people are not at home early afternoon on weekdays.

You walk several blocks before you finally see another person. Two people. A woman and a little boy playing in a yard on the opposite side of the street. As you approach, the woman lifts her hand as if to wave to you—this is, after all, a friendly place, a neighborly place—but then puts it to her mouth instead. She is looking at Walter. She reaches out and pulls the little boy close to her body. She doesn't say anything. Just holds her son and stares, as if she's unsure what to make of you and whatever it is you've got at the end of the leash.

You decide you are pleased by this reaction.

The next day, you go for another walk through the subdivision. There are a few more people out this time. No one waves, but one man does point.

On telephone poles, you take note of missing animal posters, more than you saw at the pet store. Every block seems to have a different one—pictures of kids holding kittens, small dogs curled in dog beds, one red-eyed ferret. You look to Walter and try to tell if he is familiar with these streets, or excited, filled with bloodlust perhaps. But he appears to be none of these things. Walter, in your opinion, is simply not a lustful or excitable creature.

Walks through the subdivision become part of your daily routine. You try to go at the same time each afternoon, so people can look for you if they want to look for you. Although, for the most part, no one acknowledges you. Once, an elderly woman sitting on the front porch of a house calls to Walter. "Here pretty kitty! Come here!" You lead Walter to the house and wait while the woman pets his long back and scratches under his chin. She doesn't say anything to you and the next day she isn't there.

Otherwise, it's the neighborhood's children who are most brazen, and even they keep their distance. They have a uniform, prefab quality about them, just like the homes they live in. They ride by you in packs, on shining BMX bikes, sandy hair tucked under florescent helmets. They circle the block you're walking on so they can pass by again and stare. But they never stop, never speak.

You come to see walking Walter through the subdivision as a job of sorts. It's a daily task that you cannot miss. You aren't quite sure why this is, but it's certainly a more rewarding activity than any real job you've ever held. You're outside, you're spending time with a good friend, you're getting exercise. And then, of course, you have to assume people in the subdivision have come to expect you at a certain time each afternoon. If you did not walk Walter through their neighborhood at that time, then what? You feel they need this reminder, whatever it is you and Walter are reminding them of. Perhaps only a reminder that you've got something they don't—something big, and maybe something bad. Maybe something wild.

At night, you read, or watch TV, or sketch. You continue to add your drawings to the refrigerator door and a scene develops—a forest surrounding a small house with fantastical creatures peeking in from the edges. The original sketch of Walter is at the very center. Everything circles out from him and in the drawing, he, too, looks fantastical, an image not really of this world.

The real Walter keeps you company and when you go to bed, you leave the back door open so he can go out whenever he pleases. You tell yourself you do this so he doesn't have to wake you when he needs to relieve himself. One night, you get up and look around the house for him and can't find him, but then another night you get up and he's in his favorite spot on the living room floor, so you tell yourself that other time was a fluke or just your imagination.

One night there's a knock at your door and when you go to open it, no one is there, but you can hear the giggling of kids nearby.

One night there's a knock at your door and when you open it no one is there and you hear absolutely nothing.

In the morning, you find a flier in your mailbox for a missing cat. The picture is of an obese tabby with "HAVE YOU SEEN ME?" in handwritten letters across the top. You wonder if every house on the street got one, or if this flier is just for you.

Another morning you find a different note, hand-written. "In the future, all dogs bite," it says. Though you don't know what it means, exactly, you are intrigued by the sentiment. You add it to the refrigerator door as though it were a title for the scene of your drawings.

Not long after that, something new happens. You've taken a long, looping afternoon walk through the subdivision and are on your way back toward home when Walter tugs against you on his leash. It's not a hard tug and it's not a persistent tug. Still, it's out of character. As long as you've been walking Walter through the woods and the neighborhood, he's never pulled on the leash, never tried to dictate where you go.

You assume he is tugging now because he wants to walk more. He knows from routine that you are heading home and doesn't want to go. But you're tired. You're ready to be in your house, or out on the back deck, enjoying your solitude and idleness. He tugs once more.

You decide on a compromise. What you'll do is you'll let Walter off his leash and he can walk around on his own for a bit while you watch. You've never done this before—set him loose in the neighborhood. But you can't see the harm, calm and well-mannered as he is.

"Okay, Walt," you say. "Just a few more minutes, then we head back."

It's only when you bend to release the leash clasp from Walter's collar that you see the true object of his attention. A woman standing at the end of a driveway, holding a cat. This sight stays your hand a moment. Perhaps you should not unclip the leash after all.

You're a half a block away. The woman wears high heels, slacks, a freshly ironed sweater. In the hand not holding the cat is a stack of mail. She's paused in her route from mailbox to house to examine the letter on the top of the stack. You wonder, briefly, if she carried the cat out of the house for the purpose of having company while she checked the mail, or if she simply scooped it up along the way. Regardless, the pair has caught Walter's interest.

If you set him free, that's where he'll go. You're certain of it now, this thing you've wondered about Walter for some time. Though he does not growl or lunge or bare his teeth, you can see the desire in his eyes, and in the way his stubby ears tip forward ever so slightly. That's where he'll go. Then everyone in the neighborhood's suspicions about the two of you will be confirmed. Whatever those suspicions are. You have your suspicions about their suspicions.

This particular woman is familiar to you. She might be the one who came to your house to tell you about the disappearing cats. (And here she has since found her cat. How nice for her!) Or she might be one of the women from your dream. She might even be someone you used to work with a long time ago. She doesn't see you though, and even if she did she probably wouldn't say a damn thing to you.

As the clasp clicks open in your hand, and the leash falls to your side, you tell yourself you don't know why you've done such an impulsive, foolish thing. You tell yourself you don't know what outcome you could possibly hope to see.

But you do know. You and Walter both know.

SPUD II

SPUD

July 15, 2090, Bainbridge Island, Washington
Caroline Olstead

On my way out for lunch, I stop by Angie's toll booth to see if she wants me to bring her a sandwich. She says yes, but only if it's egg salad or PB&J because she's decided she's a vegetarian again. Angie does this every couple of years. I tease her and ask if she's been talking animal rights with Spud when I'm not around. I promise egg salad and remember that I'll have to stop at the store myself since Spud never bothers to listen to messages and then I remind myself to chastise Spud for this when I get home.

I try to take a firm hand with him, like my mom did with Parker and me. It's hard to know the right way to be with Spud, though. It's a lot of pressure. Parker turned out to be a genius. An astronaut and a scientist. Spud's got the same genes, so he's got the same potential. There are so many ways Spud is already just like Parker. But I didn't raise Parker. I wasn't the one to make the hard decisions. So, when I'm stuck in any given situation, I think about what Mom would have done. I know sometimes I've got to step up and be the bad guy. In the situation of not returning a phone call and not going to the store, for example, Mom would have shouted loud enough to rattle Parker from whatever daydream he was in. You can be certain of that. So I'll take the hard line with Spud, too. Even on his birthday.

This isn't to say I want Spud to turn out to be exactly the same person as Parker. Everyone, even a clone, has the right to be whoever he wishes to be—to make his own life. It's up to Spud if he wants to be a scientist or not, an astronaut or not. That's part of the reason I try not to linger on the subject when Spud asks about his daddy. I don't want him to feel too influenced one way or the other. Like he's got to carry on in the path of some dead man he's never met.

All I mean about nurturing Spud is that Parker was so smart, and, at his core, so very kind. He really wanted to make the world a better place. Sure, we had our own challenges. When Mom was still alive, he was the good son, coming home for all the holidays. After she passed though, there was this sort of silence that cropped up between me and Parker. Not that we were mad at each other or didn't get along. We just didn't know how to be together. Like Mom had been the one thing we had in common and without her, we were strangers. He still came to visit, but less frequently, and I could tell it was mostly out of a sense of obligation, like he felt someone had to check in on lonely Caroline from time to time.

But the one thing he could get excited to talk about during those visits— if he did happen to be in a talking mood—was whatever research he was doing. He'd tell me about how marvelous the sea creatures he worked with were, and how studying them could tell humans all sorts of things about our own lives on Earth, both our past and our futures. He said knowing things like that could help us live better. I can't pretend I understood all of it. But I believe he really was doing something important. Other people thought so, too. After he died, the government sent me all kinds of awards and commendations in honor of him.

And so I'm certain Spud could turn out like that, too. If only I knew how to encourage him in the right way, and to love him in the right way, I think he could grow up to use all his brains and his sensitivities and his intuitions for good. I wish I could ask Mom, of course. But I also wish I could ask Parker. To see what he would have to say about what exactly it is Spud needs.

I do my shopping quick, and in sort of a daze, thinking about all these things. I've got a lot on my mind today. But as soon as I come up the driveway to the house, I forget all of it, scolding Spud and making cake and egg salad included. Something's wrong. First off, the stray pit bull that follows Spud around isn't sitting on the steps. Second, the front door's wide open. Of course I assume the worst.

I drop my groceries and charge in through the open door like a momma bear, hoping to startle whatever meth-head burglar's in my house. But the only person there is Spud. He's sitting at the kitchen table, hugging a bleeding arm to his chest. It looks like he's been that way for a while.

"The dog bit me," he says when he sees me.

"I can see that," I say. I'll be honest; I'm relieved. This is a Spud problem I know how to handle all on my own.

I bundle Spud's arm up in a towel and call a cab to take us to the clinic, hoping they can patch him up well enough there and we won't have to go across to the hospital in Seattle. The bridge is already absolutely miserable this time of day.

Spud bites his lip through the pain. I think of how Parker used to scream his head off every time he so much as scraped his knee. Then I think again about how there really are so many types of people Spud could turn out to be, regardless of his genes. There's no predicting the ways any given situation will shape a kid and leave a mark on him, make him different from how he could have been otherwise. It's scary, but it's kind of a big fuck-you to those scientists at the University of Michigan and all the great plans they must have had for the clones. I can't help but smile a little at the thought of it.

Tonight, I'll tell Spud how much braver he is than his daddy was at his age. How much stronger. There are other little things like that, too. I should tell him more often, whenever I notice. The scar on Spud's arm from the dog bite—that will be another thing. It'll help remind him he's his own man, even though he doesn't know enough to think otherwise.

Disruption

Each morning, a man in Detroit, Michigan pushes a button and everything falls out of my kitchen shelves and onto my kitchen floor. It is unclear to me if this is the primary function of the button or if it's simply an unintended consequence. Regardless, I find it to be an inconvenience.

This hasn't always happened. It's a fairly recent development.

I suspect the button used to do something else. It used to start an assembly line conveyor belt or open the bay doors of a warehouse. I'm certain everything would not fall out of my kitchen shelves each morning were it not for the tragic decline of the American auto industry. There are too many buttons out there no longer doing what they were designed to do.

I don't live in Detroit, Michigan. I live in Tulare, California.

Every morning, I wake up to the sound of everything on my kitchen shelves falling onto my kitchen floor. It happens at six o'clock. This is earlier than I prefer to get up. The first thing I do is I put on my slippers and robe and then I pick everything up and put it back where it belongs. Then I go online to look up phone numbers for Detroit. I am trying to find the man who pushes the button.

Each Thursday, not only does everything fall out of my kitchen shelves and onto my kitchen floor, but everything also falls out of my freezer. I am unsure if this is the result of the same button, or a separate one entirely. Since this only happens once a week, it is not an unbearable hardship. I just have to be diligent about getting out of bed quickly and returning everything to the freezer so it doesn't spoil.

I've got quite a lot of meat in my freezer. Definitely more than is necessary for one person.

I have decided it would actually be better to talk to the man who pushes the button's boss. The man who pushes the button is probably just doing his button pushing because he is paid to. I doubt he has the jurisdiction to decide whether or not the button should be pushed each morning. I wonder if he gets good health insurance and a living wage for pushing the button. I worry he may be a member of some sort of button pusher's union. If this is the case, it could be very difficult to get him to stop his work.

The man who pushes the button isn't Barrett. I could see how you might think he would be Barrett, but he isn't.

I do not ever go online and look up Barrett's phone number. I am not trying to find him.

The reason I know Barrett is not the man who pushes the button is because Barrett once said Tulare is the worst place on Earth with the exception of Detroit, Michigan and certain parts of Mexico City.

So I also know Barrett is not in certain parts of Mexico City.

I disagreed with Barrett about Tulare. In Tulare, we have a weekly farmers' market and a very nice public library. We have small town charm with big city amenities. We have beautiful natural settings within driving distance. There's even a song about Tulare, which children learn in grade school. It goes: Tulare, Tulare/Your hills and mountains cry/It's either do or die/For Tulare, Tulare/The county where the mountains meet the sky. When I told Barrett this, he said, "See, this place is so crummy even the mountains and the hills are crying."

There are a lot of songs about Detroit, including "Detroit Rock City," "Don't Stop Believing," "Motor City Madness," and "8 Mile." Sometimes I hum these songs in the morning while I clean everything off my kitchen floor and put it back on my shelves.

The number I call most often in Detroit is Directory Assistance. When the operator answers, I say, "Hello, I'm trying to find the man who pushes the button that makes everything fall out of my kitchen shelves and onto my kitchen floor." Then the operator says, "Is this a joke." I say, "No, this isn't a joke. I would also like to talk to this man's boss, if possible." Then she says, "I don't have times for jokes," and hangs up.

The number I call second most often in Detroit is the headquarters for a union that represents auto factory workers (because it turns out button pushers don't have their own union after all). When the operator answers, I say, "Hello, I'm trying to find the man who pushes the button that makes everything fall out of my kitchen shelves and onto my kitchen floor." Then the operator says, "Hi, Irene, how are you today?" I always tell her, aside from having to clean everything up off my kitchen floor, I'm all right. I say this because she sounds like a nice person and I don't want to worry her.

On Tuesdays, women from the church come over. They bring lunch and good tidings. Once, one of them told me a story about a cousin of hers whose husband disappeared and six months later the authorities called and told her he had died in Florida. She never found out the cause of death because they said she had to pay for a coroner's report and she didn't want to do that. The woman from the church told me this like she meant it to sound hopeful.

On other days, Detective Wallitsch comes over. He says, "Have you heard from him?" I tell him the truth, which is that I have not. He says, "You'll call me right away if you do." I lie and say of course I will.

Detective Wallitsch never calls before he comes over. I think this is rude. Sometimes I don't mind his stopping by. He's always very pleasant to me and does not stay long. But other times I'm busy and would prefer not to be interrupted.

For example, the first time Detective Wallitsch came over was also the first morning everything fell out of my kitchen shelves, and also out of my freezer, and onto my kitchen floor. The sound was so sudden, but also so automatic, I knew right away it was the result of someone in Detroit pushing a button. Still, I was surprised when I saw the state of the kitchen. Barrett had been gone for two days and even though I didn't know why yet, I already wasn't looking for him. There was broken glass everywhere. Now all my dinnerware is plastic. I know it isn't very classy, but it's durable. That first morning though, the mess was so bad I swapped my slippers for a pair of Barrett's boots so I wouldn't cut up my feet while I cleaned. Needless to say, that was not a convenient time for Detective Wallitsch to visit. When I answered the door, he showed me his badge and said he'd like to ask me a few questions about my husband if I didn't mind. He must have thought I was some sort of madwoman, stomping around in a robe and men's boots with my arms full of thawing meat.

Barrett and I never went to church together. If he were here, he'd say the women who come on Tuesdays are taking advantage of me. I'd ask how someone can be taking advantage if they're the ones bringing lunch. He'd say, "There's no such thing as a free lunch."

Calling the autoworkers' union has yet to lead me to the man who pushes the button. But I keep trying because I think progress is being made. The operator's name at the union is Liz and she is very helpful. The first time I called, she didn't say, "Is this a joke?" She said, "What's your name, hon?"

Liz says she doesn't think anyone affiliated with her union pushes a button that would make everything fall off the shelves and onto the floor in some lady's kitchen in Tulare, California, as that isn't exactly a productive function for autoworkers. She says it would be a waste of resources on the part of that particular plant. However, she assures me if the man who pushes the button is in fact a union member, he would be entitled to a minimum of eighteen dollars and seventy-eight per hour and if he worked more than twenty hours a week, he would have medical and dental insurance with a twenty-five dollar co-pay, a retirement plan, and an optional life insurance policy.

I tell Liz that sounds like a good job. If Barrett had a good job in Detroit pushing a button for a living wage and insurance benefits, maybe people wouldn't think he's such a bad guy.

When we'd fight, Barrett would say if he only had enough money, he'd leave and never come back. I didn't ever think he meant it though—about leaving. But then I guess there are a lot of things I didn't ever think Barrett would do.

Detective Wallitsch thinks Barrett's coming back. That's why he visits unannounced.

I don't care if Barrett comes back. But I have a fantasy where Barrett finds out about the man who pushes the button. If Barrett knew about the man who causes me such anxiety and inconvenience, maybe, just maybe, he'd drive to Detroit even though it's worse than Tulare and some parts of Mexico City and find the man himself. Maybe he'd tie the man up and also tie up the man's family. Maybe he'd hurt the man until he agreed to stop pushing the button. Maybe he'd demand the combination to the man's safe. Maybe he'd take everything of value the man had. Maybe he'd kill the man just because he felt like it. Then he'd do the same thing to the man's neighbors. This time it'd be all right because he'd have done it for me.

The reason Barrett would think the women from the church are taking advantage of me is he doesn't believe anyone ever does anything nice if it doesn't benefit them personally. That's the long version of "There's no such thing as a free lunch." Like, even if someone is helping you and it makes them feel good, that's them taking advantage. They're using you to make themselves happy. That's why, according to Barrett, selfish people are more trustworthy—at least their motives are clear.

No one has ever accused Barrett of not having a clear motive.

Liz and I don't always only talk about the man who pushes the button. Sometimes we talk about sports. Liz is a big fan of the Detroit Tigers. Sometimes we take turns listing songs about Detroit. Liz has never been to California and sometimes she asks what Tulare is like. The first time she asked, I told her Tulare County is home to Mount Whitney, which is the tallest mountain in the contiguous United States. Then I sang the song for her and said that's what they meant about the mountains reaching the sky. Unfortunately, it's the only song there is about Tulare. Liz said she thought it was nice anyway and she didn't even make a joke about the part where the hills and mountains are crying.

Tulare is also home to numerous cattle ranches and the farmers' market boasts many options for lovers of beef. Liz says she doesn't much care for beef and I agree with her. "Especially not when I have to clean it up off my kitchen floor every Thursday morning," I say. "Oh, hon," Liz says.

I suppose I don't need to keep food in the freezer at all. That would make Thursdays easier. But that's one of the things Barrett and I used to fight about. He was upset when there wasn't enough food in the house, when there wasn't enough red meat in the freezer. He accused me, from time to time, of vegetarianism, which he considered a crime. So now I try to keep plenty of things like skirt steaks and veal cutlets around, even though I don't eat that much of them myself.

I am trying to do better, is my point.

I am trying to keep a clean household, picking up everything that falls out of my kitchen shelves and onto my kitchen floor in a timely manner. I am trying to be a pleasant and cooperative citizen, telling Detective Wallitsch what he wants to hear. I am trying to be a conscientious consumer, buying lots of meat from my local farmers' market.

One thing I'm not trying to do is find Barrett. I never search for him online or call Directory Assistance in cities that aren't Detroit, Michigan or Mexico City to ask for him. I don't even read the newspaper articles about him.

But if he were to come back of his own will and volition, well, that's another story. I admitted this to one of the ladies from the church and she said, "No, not after what he did to those people," like she was making the decision for me.

Sometimes, I drive east out of town toward the hills and mountains to the Kern River. Barrett used to like to go there with me. We'd park by the river and walk through the woods or just sit in the car and look at the water. When we'd do this, I'd bully him into admitting he thought something about Tulare was nice, that he thought the river was beautiful. "Okay, okay, you win," he'd say.

Sometimes I'd bully him into admitting I was beautiful, too. "You don't have to bully me," he'd say. "You know I think you're lovely."

I don't go to the river because I think Barrett might be hiding there. Nobody thinks that. Just because Barrett likes the river doesn't make him a competent woodsman. Detective Wallitsch says that isn't even one of the places his men are looking anymore.

Sometimes, Liz calls me. Our conversations start just as they would if I called her, with her saying "Hi, Irene, how are you?" and me lying and saying I'm all right. Then we talk about the man who pushes the button, and the Detroit Tigers, and songs about Detroit, and what it's like to live in Tulare. It's comforting to catch up on our favorite topics. That Liz calls me makes me think she takes comfort in our talks, too, and I wonder what other similarities there are between us. It has occurred to me she might have misplaced someone in her life as well. Once, to broach the subject, I asked her, "Do women from the church ever bring you lunch?" She said, "No, not anymore."

Another time, Liz asked me if I might like a job working in a factory that makes cars. She said if I'd be willing to move to Detroit, she could help me get a job like that. The economy is improving, she said, and she knows of companies who would be hiring soon. She said if I moved to Detroit, I could stay with her for a little while until I found my own place. She assured me everything never falls out of her kitchen shelves and onto her kitchen floor. She said this last part like she meant it to be a joke, and although I didn't find it all that funny, given the circumstances, I appreciated the sentiment.

When I told the women from the church about Liz, they said I should accept her offer. "A change of scenery will do you good," they said. "A fresh start will do you good."

When I first told Detective Wallitsch about Liz, he said I should not accept her offer because he didn't want me to leave. Using me as bait is part of his strategy for catching Barrett. But then later he called and said, "You should go. We can always bring you in for the trial. If there's ever a trial." This made me think he doesn't actually believe Barrett is coming back after all.

I can't ask Barrett what he thinks about Liz, but I guess I know what he would say.

I think about Liz's offer while I drive, while I sit by the river and look at the hills and mountains, and while I browse the butcher stalls at the farmers' market. It's a big decision, just to pick up and go. Sometimes I envy Barrett and his success in that capacity.

Sometimes, I think about all the buttons I push during the course of a normal day. There are buttons on my keyboard, buttons on my phone, buttons on my dashboard. A button turns on my desk lamp. I wonder if, when I push these buttons, in addition to doing the things I intend them to do (search for phone numbers, call Detroit, etc.), they also do other things. I wonder if somewhere, maybe Mexico City, some woman's kitchen falls apart every time I turn on my lamp.

Then I wonder if maybe everything that happens to us is just the result of someone we don't know, in some city we've never been to, pushing buttons. A button for the women from the church to make lunch. A button for Detective Wallitsch to visit with more questions. A button for me to call Liz and ask about people pushing buttons. A button for Barrett to become a monster.

A button for Barrett to come back. A button for everything to return to the way it was, or even better than it was. A magical, time-travel, fairy-tale, wish-upon-a-star button.

The women from the church want to know what I'm waiting for. "You've got a place to stay. You've got a chance for a good job," they say.

I'm waiting because I'm worried about whatever it is that makes Detroit, Michigan worse than Tulare, California. I'm worried if I go, there'll be no hills and mountains. I'm worried there'll be no river.

I'm worried Barrett will come back while I'm gone and find a big mess. Everything from the kitchen shelves on the kitchen floor. Everything from the freezer on the kitchen floor. All of it, everything, spoiled.

SPUD I

SPUD

May 22, 2077, Outer Space
Lieutenant Colonel Parker Timothy Olstead

It's been eighteen hours since the space shuttle lost central power. And the backup backup fuel cell has also since cashed out. Of course it did. In hindsight, he thinks he knew it would. Maybe part of him even hoped for it. The chance to be valiant on the high seas. To go down with the ship.

No, that's a lie. He couldn't have wanted such a thing. He's not the sort of man who would want such a thing. Never has been.

What he wants is love and safety and comfort. Just like every other person on Earth or beyond who is not a historical sea captain. He wants familiarity and family. To feel known. To be alive and home.

In the past, when he imagined a full system failure, he'd pictured the space shuttle getting colder and colder in the dark. He imagined his eyelashes freezing, and his fellow astronauts huddling together for warmth. But of course, when he thought about it rationally, he always knew this was not the case. Instead, the Krona Ark III has become a sauna—a tiny airtight canister filled with three moving, breathing, sweating humans. Together they create a terrible heat.

He was right about his colleagues huddling together though. In the dark, he can hear the Swedes fucking. He can't tell if they are in their bunk or simply at the other end of the main cabin. In the dark and stagnant air, all sounds push together. He tries to remember if he noticed anything romantic between Edvard and Annika before the launch. He would like to know if they were already lovers or if the approach of death has made them so.

He grasps on to the console that contains his squid tanks and listens to the creatures moving, though he cannot see them. He considers masturbating. The Swedes are on to something here, he thinks, though it isn't a final sexual release he wants. It's a connection. An understanding, even brief and fleeting. He considers pulling his prized Nordic squid from its tank and holding it to his chest. But he doesn't want to frighten the squid—doesn't want it to know it should be frightened. So instead he stays perfectly still, breathes slow, and thinks of his own body taking shape a second time in the lab in Michigan.

Mr. Stills' Squid Days

Dahlia's dream is also a memory. In the dream, Dahlia is a child, and she is at the beach. She is sitting with legs thrust out to the side, half buried in the warm sand. All around her, other kids laugh and scream, running in and out of the waves, circling and zig-zagging, all trying to get close, but not too close, to the objects of their fascination. But Dahlia stays put. Then all of a sudden—as is often the case in dreams, and in reality for children too small to determine their own fates—Dahlia is up in the air. She has been scooped up by strong arms. She is being held and carried.

"You looked like you could use a ride, missy," the man with the arms says.

In the dream, Dahlia has been waiting for this. This is the best part. This is Mr. Stills.

"Let's get closer so you can see," Mr. Stills says.

He is a tall man and in his arms, Dahlia feels she is very high up. It is such a different perspective than she normally has on the world. Some children would be scared by this sudden change in altitude, but not Dahlia. She looks at Mr. Stills' curly knots of brown hair and his big smile, and feels confident that she is safe in his grasp. She breathes him in and he smells like the ocean.

Dahlia is perched up on Mr. Stills' shoulders now—so broad, they are like bench seats for tiny Dahlia—and what she sees are men in rubber boots all up and down the shore. Some are bent over, some upright, arms outstretched. Below the men are the squid. The squid lie in wet sand, helpless. These men reach for the squid, then throw them as far as they can into the cold blue water. Their movements are smooth—like the men, all working together, are a machine. In this way, they are clearing the sand of the poor, displaced creatures. Mr. Stills explains that he and his crew will stay here as long as it takes, until all the squid are back in the bay where they belong. Dahlia looks behind her and sees the children, still running and laughing, daring each other to touch the squid. Beyond that, music, magicians, vendors selling food—fried squid bites and ink pops. It is a festival, a party, this special day once a year when the men come to throw the squid. Dahlia's family is up there on the beach, somewhere, and she strains to see them, but can't pick them out so she turns her attention back to the men and their work, the way they hold each squid so gently, swinging it down toward their waists then up, then letting go at just the right moment, sending it flying. A dozen squid at a time, sailing in beautiful arcs back to their home in Monterey Bay.

When Dahlia wakes, it's the feeling of being held that lingers. Dahlia has not been held in a very long time, not since her husband, Terry, passed away more than a decade ago. Even then, Terry never held her like that. Terry was also a big man, a strong man, but he was always so cautious when picking Dahlia up. Even when he was being playful, he was cautious. Her father was the same way, and her younger brother Isaac, once he got big enough to pick her up, clumsy about it. That was always the way with any others who had ever held her: cautious or clumsy. No one was ever as cavalier, or as graceful, as Mr. Stills.

Dahlia remains in bed for a long time, replaying the dream-memory in her mind, willing her body to feel the firmness of Mr. Stills' grip around her waist, the warmth of the sun on her face, the irritating pricks of the sand pressed into her palms. It's only when she hears Madison rustling around in other parts of the house that Dahlia pulls on her robe and maneuvers herself out of bed and into her wheelchair.

In the kitchen, Madison sits hunched over a bowl of cereal, reading the newspaper. Her stringy, black bangs shag over her eyes. There's a bowl and spoon set out for Dahlia too, though Madison does not bother to greet her.

"Have I ever told you about Squid Days?" Dahlia asks as she pours milk into her bowl.

Madison shakes her head without looking up from her newspaper.

"When I was a little girl, there was this wonderful festival each year on Cowell Beach. My family went every time. There was food and music and all sorts of entertainment. It's too bad they don't have anything like it anymore. You probably would have enjoyed it."

"Probably not," Madison mumbles and Dahlia is reminded how few things Madison allows herself to really enjoy.

"Regardless, it was quite the spectacle," Dahlia says.

They eat in silence after that. The shades in the kitchen are drawn, but light still shines through and Dahlia can tell it will be a nice day. She listens for the ocean, just two blocks away, but can make out only the noise of passing traffic—a motorcycle, a city bus, the high-pitched voices of children in a pack walking past the house on their way to school. Their chattering sounds just like the children playing on the beach in her dream-memory, though those children would all be as old as Dahlia now. Dahlia thinks it would be nice to find one of those grown children and reminisce about the oddity and wonder of Squid Days. It's been so long since she's even thought of the event, much less spoken to someone about it. She can't remember how long. But it would be nice to do that today, she thinks, with the images from the dream still fresh and glorious in her mind.

"I'd like to come with you to campus this morning," Dahlia says when she's finished her breakfast. "I want to send an e-mail to Isaac."

Madison shakes her head. "I've got English then econ then I'm meeting with some people to work on a group project."

Dahlia stares back at the younger woman. She doesn't know what this has to do with her e-mailing Isaac.

"So you'll be stuck in the library all day," Madison says. "Do you want to be stuck in the library all day?"

"I don't mind."

"Fine. Can you be ready to leave in fifteen minutes? I don't want to be late."

Madison is Dahlia's grandniece. She is nineteen years old and lives with Dahlia rent-free in exchange for helping Dahlia with tasks she can't do herself, like driving, grocery shopping, the lifting of heavy objects, the cleaning of awkward spaces, etc. Helping Dahlia used to be Madison's grandmother, Joanie's, chore, but Joanie was diagnosed with type II diabetes the previous winter and is now unwell herself much of the time. When Madison is not at school, or at home with Dahlia, she is often with Joanie. And so Dahlia does not begrudge Madison her surly disposition, her near-constant bad mood. It is unfair for a young woman to have to spend so much of her free time with old women, particularly in this day and age when there are so many more exciting options for recreation.

But then, Dahlia sometimes wonders if Madison might still be angry even if she had no family obligations at all. Dahlia sometimes wonders if Madison is simply an angry person. There's a degree to which angst is fashionable among the young. To accentuate this image, Madison dyes her hair black and wears dark make-up and dark clothes most of the time, baggy black pants cascading over black boots. When Madison was in high school, her friends looked this way, too, but now Dahlia has noticed that the handful of other girls Madison associates with have cast off their black wear for jean shorts and college t-shirts or even sundresses. Short hair seems all the rage this season, red or blond. Dahlia wonders why Madison has not made this transition with her peers.

In the car, Madison listens to a grating, guttural kind of rock music, too harsh and turned up too loud for Dahlia's liking. Soon though Dahlia stops noticing the music. She looks out the window of the car and is swept up by the sunny beauty of the city she's lived in all her life. The freeway and the shopping centers and the tangle of cars, buses, bicycles on seemingly every street are new, but the sky and the water and the trees are just the same. The beaches and the boardwalk and the big wooden roller coaster. Dahlia thinks again about the excitement of Squid Days and smiles to herself.

At the community college, Madison parks in the handicapped spot in front of the library and helps Dahlia up the ramp to the front door. "I'm done at three," she says, then turns and walks quickly back down the ramp. Dahlia watches for a moment as Madison slouches across campus, head down, shoulders rounded, and wishes she could be the one to lighten the burden for her grandniece, rather than just another obligation, weighing her down, pushing her in to herself.

Dahlia likes the college library and doesn't mind the prospect of spending her day there. The facility isn't particularly impressive, but it is pleasant. There are windows on all sides and there's a coffee shop at one end of the building where she can get a sandwich or a pastry without too much fuss. Also, she is not the oldest or the most disabled person to use the library. There is often a quadriplegic woman sitting near the front entrance who Dahlia nods to when she passes. And once she saw a man who had to be at least ninety hunched over a stack of books at a study table. Dahlia doesn't know if these people are students themselves, or, like her, relatives of students who have simply stowed them in the library for a while. Either way, she feels she's in good company.

As she makes her way to an empty computer station, a work-study student rushes over to move the swivel chair out of the way for her. Dahlia thanks the young man, settles herself in front of the machine, and logs in to her Hotmail account. It's just in the last few months she has learned how to use the Internet. She's a quick typist from her days as a secretary, but she's never been one for keeping up with technology. It was Madison who set her up with e-mail and showed her how to use Web browsers, saying, "Jesus, Dahlia, it's 2003. You need to catch up," and now Dahlia feels fairly comfortable with the whole arrangement, which she knows is better than a lot of people of her generation. She takes pride in that.

There isn't much e-mail waiting for her. Just a couple of forwarded jokes from Joanie—dumb things Dahlia usually doesn't read. She asked Madison about these joke e-mails once and Madison told her to just reply "LOL" to each one. "It means 'laughing out loud.' Then you don't have to read them, but she thinks you did." But today Dahlia doesn't even bother with the LOLs. Instead, she writes to Isaac.

> Dear Isaac,
>
> This morning I had a dream about Squid Days and it was so vivid and beautiful, I had to tell you about it. Do you remember Squid Days? It stands out as one of the few events you, me, Mommy, and Daddy could all enjoy. Were we really so different, the four of us, that it took thousands of squid washing up on Cowell Beach to bring us together? I suppose we were. In the dream, Mr. Stills made a special trip to our beach blanket to pick me up and take me down to the water so I could see the men throwing the squid. Do you remember Mr. Stills? He was always such a kind man. You were not in the dream, but I thought you might appreciate it none-the-less.
> Your loving sister,
> Dahlia

She could just call Isaac to talk about Squid Days, but Isaac, a lawyer in New York (still practicing at sixty-eight, more likely to die than to retire) often uses the time difference and his hectic work schedule as excuses not to answer when Dahlia phones. And also not to return her messages. It seems to Dahlia that she and her sibling have always communicated better in writing than in person. Somehow, it's easier for both to say what they mean in notes, letters, and postcards, with no risk of being interrupted mid-thought by the other's voice. And so, these days, they talk mostly by e-mail.

After she's finished writing, Dahlia browses for books. She finds a display of items on local interest. There's one book on the history of the Santa Cruz Beach Boardwalk and another on surf culture. Both show old pictures of crowds gathered at Cowell Beach, children playing in the surf, and families on beach blankets. But neither mentions Squid Days, or squid at all for that matter.

An hour later, Dahlia gets back on the computer and sees Isaac has responded to her e-mail. His note is brief.

> Sorry, Sis, no idea what you're talking about with the Squid Days or this Mr. Stills fellow. No recollection. Your dream sounds nice though. My regards to Joanie and Maddy. Be well. –Ike

So Isaac doesn't remember. But Dahlia remembers Isaac in his bright blue bathing trunks and sun hat, sitting in the sand, ink pop in one hand, plastic shovel in the other, digging and sucking, his lips an ink-stained smile. A fussy toddler, he was his happiest at Squid Days.

Dahlia knows Isaac's response shouldn't surprise her. Indeed, throughout her life, her brother seems to have made it a point to always disappoint, or undermine, or side-step Dahlia somehow. Why should this be any different? Yet, she had so hoped he'd be willing to share in her recollection of Squid Days! She wants someone to join her in the memories of this magical event, so many years in the past—to agree with her that, yes, Squid Days was truly something special, and what a shame it no longer takes place. She knows she can't talk about it with just anyone. It's too strange a vision, and too far removed from the modern day realities of Cowell Beach—burrito shacks and boogie board rental shops and a peculiar smell, not as bad as rotten eggs, but similar—for most to appreciate. She needs someone who was there. Really, Dahlia thinks, her brother should be that person. Dahlia decides she will try Isaac again the following day. Perhaps it is simply a matter of providing more detail to ignite in him some spark of reminiscence.

But the next morning, Madison is gone before Dahlia gets up. There's a note on the table that says "Went to school early to study." This means Dahlia will have to take the bus downtown to the public library if she wants to write to Isaac again.

Strangely, though almost everyone at the public library on a weekday morning is Dahlia's age (if not older), she's less comfortable there than at the community college. There's this feeling of time being wasted, as if everyone is just counting the minutes until they can go somewhere else. Dahlia does not like this feeling. She much prefers the studious, focused atmosphere of the college. She finds an open computer and responds to Isaac's e-mail from the day before.

> Dear Issac,
>
> Oh, I do wish you'd make an effort to recall Squid Days! I suspect you'll find it there, somewhere in the recesses of your brain, if you really try. I have a picture in my mind (as clear as if it were a photograph!) of you reaching out like you wanted to catch each squid with your tiny hands before the men could throw them back in the sea. You were so fascinated by all the goings-ons there at the beach. Once, a magician came up to us and made a small wooden carving of a squid appear behind your ear. Daddy paid him a dime so you could keep it. Does none of this ring any bells? Do let me know.
>
> Fondly,
>
> Dahlia

She hits the "Send" button. But in her heart, she knows Isaac will still not give her the response she wants. He won't even consider it. In true little brother fashion, even if he does remember Squid Days, he'll deny, deny, deny, until empirical evidence forces him to admit he is wrong. It's so silly, Dahlia thinks, this lifelong rivalry. But she's not above it herself. She decides she will find proof of Squid Days and send it to Isaac. She'll force him to say she's right about Squid Days—that he was there, that he remembers, and that he liked it.

She starts with an Internet search, but finds nothing corresponding to "Santa Cruz Squid Days," or even just "Squid Days." Searches for "Squid in Monterey Bay" yield a plethora of results, but not the thing she's looking for. She tries the library's own card catalogue, unsure what books might be of use. She decides, ultimately, that newspaper clippings are the best, something proclaiming "Squid Days Is On Its Way!" in bold block script.

She flags down a library aide, a young volunteer from the local high school, and asks for help accessing the microfiche collection. She doesn't tell the girl exactly what she's looking for, only that she wants old articles about squid in the Monterey Bay. She doesn't want to sound batty, talking about some weird beachside squid party from the olden days. So she keeps it simple. The girl gets Dahlia set up with the machine and brings her a reel of microfilm with a story about a squid fisherman who was killed in a bar fight in 1939 and several about the impact of pollution on the bay's marine life. But no Squid Days. Dahlia shakes her head. "No, I'm afraid this isn't quite right," she says to each article.

"I'm sorry we couldn't find what you were looking for," the young library aide says after twenty minutes, signaling to Dahlia this project has exhausted her patience. Before she returns to the reference desk though, the aide mentions to Dahlia that the university has a marine lab out by Natural Bridges State Beach.

"They do all kinds of research about the animals that live in the bay," she says. "So you might try them with your questions."

Dahlia decides that's exactly what she'll do. A trip out to Natural Bridges seems like a lot of effort just to prove her brother wrong. But Dahlia doesn't like to give up on a project once she's started. She'll get her proof of Squid Days; she's certain it's just a matter of looking in the right place. She thanks the aide for her help and for the information about the lab.

Across the road from the bus station, the protestors are out, waving their signs that say "No More Blood For Oil," and "U.S. Out of Iraq," and "Regime Change Starts At Home." It seems to Dahlia they're there almost every afternoon and she's glad for this. She herself is not in favor of the war. She worries, though, that these particular protestors—mostly students from the university—lack a sense of history, and what good is political action if it takes no heed of what came before it? At least, that's Dahlia's feeling.

Once, she tried to engage the protestors in conversation, telling them her husband had died in the first Gulf War. But this information only seemed to baffle them and she could not tell if it was because they couldn't see how the first Gulf War connected to the current one, or because they assumed her far too old to have lost a spouse in combat just twelve years prior. And it was true that Terry hadn't died in combat, per se. He was an engineer whose company had been contracted by the Pentagon to design portable plumbing and irrigation systems that could be easily assembled at bases in the desert without much know-how on the part of those assembling them. He was touring an army camp in Kuwait when he'd suffered an embolism and died. He was sixty-two years old, leaving Dahlia a widow at the same age.

So now she doesn't say anything as she passes the protestors on her way to the bus, but she does offer a quick thumbs up, which is returned by a skinny boy in ripped corduroy shorts with natty, knotted hair.

When the bus driver sees Dahlia, he lowers the bus's wheelchair ramp and comes out to help her up and secure her and her chair into a space in the front. He chatters away in a false-friendly voice as he does this. His yammering is mostly about the weather, and then also something about birds. Dahlia isn't sure if he's talking to her, as though she were a child, or talking at her, as though she were a piece of luggage. Dahlia smiles back and acts as if what the driver is saying is all part of a perfectly normal adult conversation. She offers the periodic "Is that so?" and "How interesting" until he's done and then she thanks him for his help. She could be rude. She could embarrass the man by haughtily stating that just because she's in a wheelchair that doesn't make her dumb. But Dahlia's never been that way with anyone. She knows it's a little cliché, but she always says her philosophy is just to treat others the way she wants them to treat her and hope they catch on. Like with the bus driver. Except he doesn't catch on, and the whole charade repeats itself when the bus stops at the marine lab ten minutes later and Dahlia has to be unloaded.

The marine lab actually has two entrances—one for a small museum and aquarium whose sign proclaims "Open to the Public" in bright orange letters, and one for the laboratory whose sign does not stipulate who it is and is not open to. Dahlia picks the latter.

Inside, the lab is really just one big room, sectioned into clusters of tables and equipment, hardly any of which is in use. There's a strange quiet to the place. A young woman working a desk near the door notices Dahlia and stands to greet her. She looks like Madison, with her stringy dyed-black hair and excessive facial piercings. But her expression is kind.

"Can I help you?" she asks.

Dahlia is unsure where to start. Here in the lab, she feels her purpose should be more scientific than personal. She says she's looking for information about squid migration patterns—historical information, if possible. Have the bay's squid populations decreased in recent decades? Was there ever a spike in the population, perhaps for even just a few years in the 1930s?

The girl shakes her head, says she doesn't know the answers to any of it. Her research concentration is in salmon, primarily, she explains.

"But you might ask Cyril," she says. "He's our cephalopod man."

She points toward a sturdy-looking young man wearing a lab coat that's clearly too tight on him. He sits with his back to them on the other side of the room and the girl offers to escort Dahlia, but Dahlia declines. She doesn't want to tax the girl's kindness. She knows how quickly that sort of thing can happen.

She motors up to the table where the young man is hunched, looking at slides and making furious notes on a laptop computer.

"I'm told you're someone who can answer my questions about squid," Dahlia says.

"Is that so?"

Dahlia looks around, afraid she may have approached the wrong person. But there's no one else in the lab.

"You're Cyril, right?"

"Yeah. What's your squid question?"

His face has the quality of being both boyish and severe at the same time. He's got freckles, a mop of curly hair, and wide puppy dog eyes set a little too close together. But he's also got a square jaw that perfectly matches a set of broad, square shoulders just below. He reminds Dahlia of the Rock'em Sock'em Robot toys Madison loved as a child. No wonder he looks uncomfortable in his lab coat. This young man is not built for science.

He doesn't smile. This surprises Dahlia. Normally strangers smile when she talks. Sometimes these smiles seem genuinely friendly, but more often they're patronizing, like the bus driver and the library aide. Regardless, they're something Dahlia is accustomed to. This unsmiling face unnerves her and she finds herself flustered. She tries to say again what she said to the girl with the piercings, that she's curious about seasonal swells in the squid population. Was it possible that sometimes there were so many squid that some would beach themselves in confusion? That hundreds of squid would beach themselves? Maybe this doesn't happen anymore, she says, in fact she's certain it doesn't happen anymore. But it used to happen and what would have been the cause of that?

Cyril shakes his head. "I'm not really sure what you're asking me," he says.

Dahlia takes a deep breath and tries again. "When I was a little girl, every year in the summer squid would suddenly wash up on the sand at Cowell Beach. Men from the community went down to the shore to help them by throwing them back into the water. There was a festival that went along with it called Squid Days, which was organized by a man named Mr. Stills. People from all over town would come to watch. I know it seems strange, but I remember everyone enjoying it quite a bit, my own family included."

Finally, Cyril does smile, though only a little.

"That sounds like something I'd very much like to see," he says.

"But I was so young at the time," Dahlia says. "There's a lot I can't recall. So I'm trying to find out more about it."

Cyril tells Dahlia he'll ask around the department and see if anyone's ever heard of anything like what she's described. He asks for the best way to get a hold of her and she gives him her e-mail address. She could give him a phone number, but she badly wants this young man's help. There's something about him—his bulk, and his no-nonsense attitude—that appeals to Dahlia. He seems maybe even a little Mr. Stills-like in these ways. And so, it is important to Dahlia that he take her seriously. It is important to her that he knows she is the sort of woman who can communicate by e-mail. He, in turn, gives Dahlia a business card identifying him as a graduate student assistant in marine biology, his own personal e-mail address written on the back.

At home that evening, Dahlia is enthused about her progress, happy to have enlisted Cyril's help in her quest for information. She's almost forgotten her original reason for trying to find proof of Squid Days—to spite Isaac—and now feels genuinely caught up in the research for its own sake. It's strange that something so vivid in her memory has seemingly been erased from Santa Cruz history. She wants to know why. She feels like Indiana Jones, digging through the rubble for something valuable and lost.

Over dinner, she chatters away about Squid Days, having forgotten her concern that someone who was not there could not possibly understand it. After all, Cyril seemed to understand just fine. She tells Madison about the beauty of the men working together on the shore, the way they threw each squid so gracefully, like they were doing a dance. She talks about all the treats at the food vendor carts and how everyone in her family, especially Isaac, loved the sweet, runny ink pops the best. She tells Madison about the kindness of Mr. Stills, how he wanted everyone to enjoy Squid Days, how every year he made sure Dahlia got to ride on his shoulders down to the water so she could see with her own eyes the magic of the men throwing the squid.

"Jesus, Dahlia," Madison interrupts, shaking her head, her mouth twisted in either concern or frustration, or both. "Tell me you haven't told anyone else about this Squid Days thing."

Dahlia lies and says she has not.

Dahlia's dream is also a memory, but this time, the dream is different. Again, she is a little girl in the sand with her useless legs half buried. Somewhere nearby, Isaac is sitting in Mother's lap, munching on squid snacks. All around, children with regular legs run like tops in stupid circles but Mr. Stills does not pick them out. Just as before, he comes only to Dahlia and scoops her up without asking. She squeals in surprise and delight. Again, he carries her on his broad shoulders to the water's edge so she can watch the men throwing squid, the creatures strangely graceful in flight.

What is different in this dream is that the other men are not standing on the shore. They are out in the bay on boats. They are reaching into the water and pulling squid out, then tossing them onto the beach. They're not saving the squid; they're killing them. Dahlia isn't upset by this though. It's all part of Squid Days. It's the biggest day of the year for the town's fishing industry. She turns to see the magicians and the food vendors and the running, screaming children. She looks back at the bay. The men on the boats stay small in the distance, but the squid get bigger as they fly toward the shore.

Awake, in bed, Dahlia wonders about Mr. Stills. She has no memory of him outside of Squid Days. But in the context of Squid Days, he was always the man of the hour. He was in charge, overseeing everything, coordinating the vendors and the fishermen alike. She's not sure how she knows this, exactly. She has no recollection of being told as much. She can't remember anyone ever saying anything specific to her about Mr. Stills, and yet, she is certain he was someone all the other grown-ups held in high regard. She can almost hear her father, in his gravelly voice, saying, "That Stills, now there's a man who gets things done."

And then there's the question of how Mr. Stills knew to seek out Dahlia. Dahlia tries to remember this as well, but can't be certain. Was he a neighbor? A member of her family's church? Or had he simply seen her chair lying in the sand and sensed that here was a little girl who might like to see the squid, but could not make it to the water's edge under her own power? And then, so thoughtful, he remembered to look for the same little girl each year after. Dahlia wonders if maybe Mr. Stills even had a young relative of his own who was in a wheelchair. A niece or a daughter perhaps. And so he knew how to offer attention in a way that made Dahlia feel she was worthy not just because her legs didn't work but because she herself was a very special person. Like her legs, working or not, didn't matter at all. That's the way she felt, too, when she first met Terry. She remembers how he smiled wide whenever she talked, but not in that patronizing way most people smiled. How he'd sometimes get so excited when he was walking beside her chair, chattering away, trying to impress her, that he'd speed up and actually leave her behind. She'd have to call after him, laughing, "Terry, wait for me." And he'd come slinking back to her side, embarrassed, but still smiling.

Funny, Dahlia thinks, how some men know instinctively just the right way to be, even if they don't know they know it.

The fact that the dream that is also a memory has changed does not bother Dahlia. Memory is, after all, fallible. But the feeling of Squid Days— sun, sand, Mr. Stills—remains consistent. And that, she thinks, is the most important thing.

All the same, Dahlia knows the images from this most recent dream will impact her search for information about Squid Days. Cyril won't be able to help her if he doesn't know what he's looking for. At breakfast, she tells Madison she wants a ride out to the marine lab by Natural Bridges. She says she can be ready to go right away if Madison is worried about being late for class.

"They have an exhibit at the museum I'm very interested in," Dahlia says. She doesn't want to be caught in her lie from the previous night, and also doesn't want to worry Madison more than she already has. And so, she lies again.

As usual, Madison's facial expression conveys disapproval.

"It's about squid," Dahlia says. She has found the best lies often require a little bit of truth.

"Just to look and see," she adds. "There's no harm in learning a little bit about them, I don't think."

Madison's expression doesn't change. "Okay," she says. "I can take you if we leave RIGHT NOW. But I don't want this to become a whole big thing."

Dahlia promises it will not become a whole big thing, whatever that might mean.

At the marine lab, Madison helps Dahlia to the entrance and tells her she'll be back at noon to pick her up. Dahlia waits until the car is out of sight before she goes inside, to the laboratory not the museum.

Once again, it's the young woman with the black hair and piercings who greets her.

"Back again, eh?" she asks, her voice high and cheerful.

"Yes. I don't mean to be a bother, but I'd like to speak with Cyril."

"No bother at all. I'm just waiting for my data to aggregate anyway," she gestures to a computer behind her where numbers seem to spill down the screen in no particular order. "It's pretty boring right now, but in a few more hours I'll be up to my eyeballs in annual spawning trends. Cyril just went out to smoke. I'm sure he'll be back in a sec."

Then, as if on cue, the side door to the lab swings open, banging against the interior wall.

"Cyril, jeez, that's so loud," the girl says.

"Sorry," he mutters.

Cyril gives Dahlia the exact same look as when he first saw her the day before. Clear-eyed and grim-faced. No smile. It's a strange way to be looked at, to be sure. Dahlia worries he is somehow irritated with her, angry even. She is about to apologize, but he speaks first.

"I'm sorry. I don't have any information for you yet. I haven't had time."

Very business-like. Dahlia respects this. She suspects this is meant to be the end of the brief conversation, but she persists. She assures him that's fine. In fact, she has new information that might spare him some misguided research. Then she waits. Finally, Cyril shrugs.

"Okay. Come over here and we can talk." He points to the lab table where Dahlia found him yesterday. She follows him across the room, the tinny sound of her chair's electric motor seems extra loud in such a big space. And then when she stops, it's as if there's no sound in the room at all.

Cyril glances back toward the young woman with the piercings like he doesn't want their conversation to be overheard. He's not irritated, Dahlia realizes. He's embarrassed. But who is he embarrassed for? Himself or Dahlia? She can't tell.

"I did ask my advisor and another professor if they'd ever heard of anything like what you described. They said they hadn't. They said it really doesn't seem like something that could have happened, knowing what we do about squid behavior in the bay." He looks down at her over the bridge of his glasses while he says this, like he's a doctor offering her a diagnosis. "They suggested... maybe you weren't remembering it correctly."

Dahlia nods. She knows what he really means by this—that the whole story is so odd, it couldn't have happened. It is only the failings of an old, decrepit mind. But Squid Days did happen. Dahlia is sure of it, even though the dream-memory has changed. She refuses to acknowledge any other possibility.

"Yes, that's exactly what I wanted to tell you," Dahlia says, plunging forward. "I wasn't remembering it correctly. I said that men came to the beach to toss squid back into the bay for Squid Days, but now I'm certain it was the other way around. Men went out on boats to fish for the squid and then when they caught them, they tossed them *onto* the beach. It was really a tremendous amount of squid."

"Yeah. My advisor suggested maybe it happened somewhere else. Is that possible?"

Dahlia says it is not. She's lived in Santa Cruz her whole life.

"Me, too," Cyril says. The first piece of personal information he's volunteered, Dahlia notes.

"Is that why you chose to study squid?" Dahlia thinks again about Cyril's resemblance to Mr. Stills. Perhaps his legacy runs through this young man in some way.

"I've just always been fascinated by all marine life," he says.

"Because you grew up by the bay?"

"Yeah. Because I grew up by the bay and I thought about the whole world of plants and animals that live there but that we don't even see most of the time. I like getting to see them now." He looks down at his hands when he says this, like he's, again, a little embarrassed. There's a hint of self-consciousness in him Dahlia had not seen during their first meeting. She decides it's a likable quality.

"How did you get here, anyway?" Cyril asks, as if he's only just realized the inconvenience of the marine lab's location for someone like Dahlia.

"My grandniece drives me wherever I need to go. Although yesterday I took the bus. She'll be back at noon to get me."

"In the future, maybe you could just call. Save yourself the trip."

Dahlia accepts this rebuke. The marine lab is not her private research facility. Cyril is busy and doesn't need to be interrupted by Dahlia everyday.

"Yes, of course. I'll do that." She's turns her chair to leave, but Cyril stops her.

"Well, hey, you don't have to run off right away," he says.

Cyril tells her it's okay with him if she wants to stay in the lab until Madison comes back. She thanks him. She asks if there's a computer she can use while she waits. He sets her up at a desk next to his and shows her how to access the university library's online databases, which he tells her will let her search through scholarly works, not just what's on the Web, and again she is grateful for his knowledge and his help.

She spends the rest of her time in the lab looking for information about Mr. Stills. She and Cyril don't speak much, except once when he asks if she'd like a cup of coffee and she declines, but she likes working next to him. His posture and focus are so studious. It makes her feel like her own research is, by extension, equally as important.

Dahlia learns there are three Stills families in the Santa Cruz area, but finds nothing about their involvement in any squid-related activities. She does come across an article in a journal devoted to nineteenth century oral history that tells a story of a man named Josiah Stills who, shortly after the incorporation of Santa Cruz as a city in 1876, single-handedly laid nine miles of railroad tracks to connect Santa Cruz to the nearby seaside town of Capitola. Sadly, this Stills was never able to acquire a train to run on his tracks as neither city wanted to finance such a project.

The article provides the story as an example of folk legends from the region. Dahlia, however, prefers to believe it's true. Certainly no one would attempt such a thing today, but she likes to think there was once a time when an industrious man really could build his own rail line, bolstered only by brute strength and the blind optimism that if he set down the track, a train would be provided.

Dahlia knows her willingness to believe such a story puts her in the minority. Certainly many people, younger people in particular, would dismiss it as a tall tale. She thinks again about how the kids of Madison's generation lack a sense of history. She suspects this is, in part, why Madison was so alarmed by Dahlia's account of Squid Days the night before. If you refuse to acknowledge that the place you live was once very different from how it is now, stories from the past will seem upsetting, and those who tell them will sound like kooks. Though who could blame Madison, or her peers, for harboring such biases? It's considerably easier to say that an old person with a strange story has lost their mind, than to consider the possibility that the world has changed so much in just a few decades.

When Madison comes to pick her up, Dahlia is waiting outside in the shade of an oak tree. She feels compelled to account for her time. She tells Madison that the squid exhibit was very informative and she went through it twice.

"And they have a computer for anyone to use," she says. "I did e-mail and read the news."

Madison, however, does not seem to care.

In the car, Dahlia sinks into the gut-heavy music and the view passing outside the window of the car, allowing herself to be lulled into an almost meditative state. So it is doubly surprising to her when Madison asks, "What's an ink pop?"

The question is so strange out of context, Dahlia almost laughs. She wonders how long Madison has been thinking of ink pops, trying to piece together an image. Her first instinct is to ask Madison what *she* thinks an ink pop is and then tell her she's correct, whatever her answer is for no other reason than to be allowed a moment's insight into the girl's mind.

"They're popsicles made of squid ink."

"Gross," Madison says. "Do they taste like fish?"

"No. They taste fruity—sort of like raspberries."

Madison doesn't respond to this.

"They are black like ink though," Dahlia continues. "Little kids get the juice all over themselves. It looks like everyone's been eating Bic pens."

"Gross," Madison says again. But this time she smiles as she says it. Dahlia wonders if she's misjudged Madison. Maybe she is willing to believe in Squid Days, just a little, after all. Dahlia decides not to press the issue. It's always such a balancing act, to win Madison's favor.

This conversation gives Dahlia another idea. When they get home, she waits until Madison is tucked away in her room with the door closed and then goes to the kitchen phone. She looks in the phone book for the number of an ice cream parlor located near downtown, one of the few places still in business from when she was a child. She wonders if they may have been the original makers of the ink pops, and if so, might they be able to validate the existence of Squid Days in some way. She calls and when a young-ish sounding woman answers, Dahlia asks to speak with the person in the shop who has worked there the longest.

"That's Reed," the woman says, then there's a pause and a man's voice on the line asking what he can do for Dahlia. This man sounds hardly older than the teenager who first answered the phone. Sometimes it seems to Dahlia everyone in the whole city is under the age of twenty-five. It's no wonder no one remembers Squid Days, she thinks.

She asks if he knows if the shop ever made squid ink popsicles.

Reed laughs. "We've made ice cream out of some pretty weird things, but I've never heard of that," he says.

Dahlia thanks him anyway and wishes him a nice day.

"You, too," he says. Then he adds, "There's a stall at the farmer's market that sells squid ink pasta. But that's really all I know of."

Dahlia can't decide if she finds this information useful or not.

Almost as soon as she hangs up the phone, it rings. It happens so quickly, Dahlia wonders if it has something to do with the call she has just made; perhaps Reed, remembering some other detail about ink pops and calling her back to say so. But when she answers the phone, it's only Joanie.

Dahlia hears concern in her sister-in-law's voice. "Is Maddy there?" Joanie asks.

Dahlia says yes, and offers to go get her, but Joanie says, "No, no. It's all right. I just wanted to make sure she was there."

Dahlia is reminded of how seriously Joanie took her role as Dahlia's caretaker, back before she got sick and Madison inherited the responsibility in her place. Joanie had spent most afternoons at Dahlia's house. While she was there, Joanie assumed all tasks, even small ones Dahlia could easily do herself, like checking the mailbox or answering the phone. This is one thing Dahlia appreciates about Madison—the younger woman allows Dahlia her independence as much as possible. If nothing else, Madison is never in the way.

"Well, I was just calling to check in," Joanie says, "to make sure everything is okay. Is everything okay?"

Dahlia tells her, yes, everything is okay. Why wouldn't it be?

"To be honest, Isaac asked me to call," Joanie says. "He said he got some weird e-mails from you."

This stings. That Isaac would call Joanie—a woman who isn't even related to him (Joanie and Madison are Terry's kin), who he's only met in person a handful of times—to check in on her rather than simply calling Dahlia himself. Typical Isaac, anything to avoid having a real conversation with his own flesh and blood. Dahlia remembers her observation from her first e-mail of the week—*were we really so different?* And of course the answer is *yes*.

"Joanie," Dahlia says, "perhaps you can help me here. Do you remember ever going to any festivals at Cowell Beach when you were young?"

"We went to watch the surf contests sometimes," Joanie says. "And I remember once there was something with fireworks. For New Year's, or Fourth of July."

"What about a festival involving squid in some way?"

Joanie laughs, but her laughter has a nervous edge. And when she speaks, there's real concern in her voice. "Squid? What do you mean? Is this what you were talking to Isaac about?"

Dahlia knows she's made her sister-in-law uncomfortable, and instantly regrets it.

"Oh, well, yes, but only as a joke. I was teasing Isaac about a bit of family lore. I thought maybe I could get you in on it, as well," Dahlia says, in hopes of assuaging Joanie's fears. "But perhaps I went too far. I didn't mean to worry him. It was just a little conflict among siblings. You remember how that goes, right, Joanie?"

Now Joanie laughs again, but this time it sounds genuine. "Oh sure. I used to contradict Terry just for the sake of contradicting him. It's tough being the youngest. There was a time I would have argued the world was flat if I thought it would get his attention."

"Well, there you go."

"Sometimes I still catch myself thinking 'Oohhhh, that will really piss off Terry when I tell him.' You wouldn't think so anymore, after so long. But old habits die hard, as they say."

Dahlia suspects she may never stop thinking of things to say to Terry and then abruptly remembering she no longer can. She and Joanie have never had a lot in common, but they did both love Terry very much and so now they've got their shared grief. It's a strange, sad bond the two women share, but it's one Dahlia is grateful for. If not Joanie, who else would there be?

"Yes, I know," Dahlia says.

Joanie asks how Madison is doing. Again, there is worry in her voice. Dahlia wishes she could say Madison is thriving here in her house, coming out of her shell, finding joy in the world around her. But this is simply not the case.

"She seems to be taking school very seriously," Dahlia says, grasping for something good to share. "She's really quite dedicated to her studies. In fact, she's in her room doing homework right now."

Joanie says she's glad to hear this and talks for a bit about how she was herself quite the bookworm in her day and would have gone to college had she not been sidetracked by her early and exhausting marriage, the birth of Madison's mother when Joanie was far too young to be a good parent, divorce, and, finally, raising a grandchild by herself when her daughter abandoned the infant Madison in Joanie's care.

"Maybe Maddy will be a professor, or some kind of scientist," Joanie says.

Dahlia thinks of Cyril's colleague at the marine lab, the girl so similar to Madison in appearance, but softer in her demeanor. Maybe if Madison had something she could be passionate about, something or someone to truly care about, she could soften in this way, too.

"I think that would be lovely, yes," Dahlia agrees.

Before she hangs up, she tries once more to mine Joanie for Squid Days information, asking if her family was ever acquainted with a man by the name of Stills. It's risky to ask another weird question out of context, Dahlia knows, but Joanie does not seem thrown this time. She says no, the name is unfamiliar, but Dahlia can tell her mind is not really on the issue at hand—it's still with her granddaughter, a person who causes Joanie even greater concern than Dahlia does. She wants so much more for the girl, Dahlia knows.

After dinner that night, Dahlia asks Madison to come for a walk with her.

"Where?" Madison wants to know, her voice full of suspicion.

"Not far. Just down to the beach. I want to look at the water."

They travel the two blocks to the beach without speaking. The evening is surprisingly quiet; the only sound is the hum of Dahlia's chair. Madison walks slowly beside her, her arms crossed, head down.

When they reach the sand, Dahlia stops. The beach slopes out in front of them several hundred yards. To the west, the big wooden roller coaster—built before Dahlia was born and rimmed with what look like oversized Christmas lights—blinks, giving off a pulsing yellow glow.

"Pleasant out," Dahlia says.

Madison points down the road. "If we go a little further this way you can watch the sunset," she says.

"No," Dahlia says. "I like it here."

But Dahlia doesn't look at the water. Instead, she studies her grandniece. Madison keeps her head down and either doesn't notice Dahlia staring at her, or doesn't care. A strap has come loose from the small bag attached to the back of Dahlia's chair and Madison reaches out, seemingly instinctively, and secures it back into place, then jams both hands into her pockets. Before Madison moved in with her, Dahlia did not know it was possible for a person to be both unflaggingly dutiful and resentful at the same time.

"Madison, what would make you happy?" Dahlia asks.

"I'd like to go back and finish my homework. I have a big assignment due at the end of the week."

Typical Madison, Dahlia thinks. Refusing to consider any question beyond its most immediate, superficial meaning. Such a peculiar and passive kind of obstinance.

"I mean in general. You seem unhappy so much of the time."

"I'm not unhappy."

"But you're not happy."

"Well, nobody's really happy."

"That's not true."

"Name one person who's happy."

"I come in contact with people all the time who seem happy."

"People who *seem* happy. They're just pretending because that's how they think they're supposed to be. There's a lot of societal pressure to act happy even if you're not, you know."

"Is it boys?" Dahlia asks. "Are you having trouble with boys, I mean?"

"Jesus, no, Dahlia. It's not boys."

"Because you're really very pretty when you let yourself be. Any boy would be lucky to have you."

"Jesus," Madison mutters again.

"In fact, I recently met a very nice young man you might like. He studies marine biology at the university. Maybe I could introduce you."

"No," she says.

Dahlia scrapes some sand that has collected on the edge of her chair into her hands. She rubs her palms back and forth to feel the scratch of it. This isn't really the conversation she hoped to have with Madison.

"You know," Dahlia says, "for a long time I was very unhappy because I was lonely. I worried no one could ever fall in love with me because who would want to be with a woman in my condition? My life would always be a small, sad thing, I thought. But then I met Terry and he made me feel like I was so dumb to even think I was unlovable. All that loneliness just rushed away. And after that, I only wished I had been more patient and not spent so much time being sad. It's a hard thing, not knowing what comes next. But I think you have to trust it will be something good."

And when Madison doesn't respond to this, Dahlia adds, "That's all I wanted to say," and means it.

"Are you lonely again now that Terry's gone?" Madison asks.

The childishness of this question surprises Dahlia. As if her grandniece, in spite of her own parent-less upbringing, and her moping and angst and sad music, has never considered the implications of loss for people other than herself.

"In a way I did not think possible," Dahlia says.

She rubs her hands back and forth until she's certain the granules of sand have wedged themselves into her fingers for good and will stay with her forever. She remembers evenings on this beach with Terry. On warm nights, they would come down here together after dinner with a blanket and sometimes a bottle of wine. They'd leave Dahlia's chair on the sidewalk and Terry would carry her, gently, across the sand. Even in her prime, Dahlia never weighed more than 110 pounds and it seemed to her that big, strong Terry could have carried her like this all the way to Mexico if he'd wished. They'd pick a spot to sit and chat and watch the sunset and though it was nothing glamorous or special, just a pleasant routine, they would luxuriate in the simple joy of being with each other. This memory is certain and fixed in

Dahlia's mind. She doesn't need history books or news clippings or marine biology students to prove to her it is true.

Dahlia's dream is also a memory. Same as before, there is the sand, the sun, the laughing, teasing children. Same as before, Mr. Stills reaching for her, carrying her, as if she weighs nothing, down to the water so she can see better. The feeling of being so safe bound up in his arms, like wherever he wanted to take her that would be all right.

But this time, there are no men at all. This time, there are only the squid. Out in the bay, they leap in and out of the water. They are flying. They are dancing. Their movement seems both deliberate and purposeless at the same time. Back on the beach there are no magicians, no vendors. The other children, who are far fewer in number, limit their play to the top of the beach near the boardwalk. They do not want to get too close. There is something unnerving in the way the squid move, yanking themselves free of the water only to crash back into it seconds later, and Dahlia thinks the other kids are right to be wary. But when Mr. Stills turns like he's going to walk away from the shore to return Dahlia to where he found her, she says "no." She wants to stay longer.

Unlike the previous two dream-memories, Dahlia finds no joy in this one. Instead, she wakes with a sense of melancholy she cannot shake. It's not that she didn't enjoy the dream. But rather that its end is unbearable. There is no Mr. Stills anymore. There's no more Mother and Father. There's barely even Isaac. And if there still had been Terry, none of these other absences would be so consuming, but of course, Terry is gone, too. Dahlia feels overwhelmed by her losses, weighed down by them, and cannot get out of bed.

Outside her door, she hears Madison stomping around the house, doors opening and closing, quiet punctuated by bursts of activity. It's Saturday, the day Madison runs errands for Dahlia and also for Joanie. Dahlia knows she should catch Madison while she can and write up a grocery list for her. Otherwise Madison, left to her own devices, will bring home only cold cereal and microwave foods. But she lacks the energy.

She keeps her eyes closed and pictures the squid jumping from the bay. Why did they do that, Dahlia wonders. And if there was no real festival, then was there also no Isaac eating ink pops, no mother sitting nearby on the beach blanket? No boasting, taunting hoards of children? Perhaps, truly, they were never there at all. Perhaps it was always just Dahlia and Mr. Stills at Squid Days. There is something freeing in this thought—that Squid Days was not a shared experience, but rather something privately hers. It is possible she is the only person in Santa Cruz who knows about it because she was the only one who was there. Just her and Mr. Stills, who would certainly have long since passed away.

It's early afternoon by the time Dahlia leaves her bedroom. She finds Madison in the den on her knees, her head and torso underneath Dahlia's ancient writing desk. On top of the desk is a cream-colored computer monitor. A keyboard, mouse, and tangle of wires lie on the ground near Madison's feet.

"What's all this?" Dahlia asks.

"It's so you don't have to go all over town just to check your e-mail," Madison says.

"You bought this for me?"

"Used. It's nothing fancy, but it will do Internet stuff and word processing. I figured that's all you need, right?" Madison has extracted herself from beneath the desk. She is looking at Dahlia like she's waiting to be told she's done good. Dahlia can't remember the last time she saw Madison this way—a little girl, eager to please.

Dahlia smiles at her. "It's lovely," she says. "Thank you. Really."

Madison blushes, then quickly turns back to whatever she was doing with the wires.

"Well, like I said, it's stupid to have to go to the library or whatever for something you can do at home."

Dahlia's first e-mail sent from her new computer is to Cyril. She is embarrassed, having to write him again to correct her account of Squid Days. She worries he really will begin to think her demented, if he doesn't already. But she also figures Cyril can't find information about Squid Days if he doesn't know what he's looking for. It is important to be as accurate as possible.

Dear Cyril,

It appears I might once again have been wrong about the annual Squid Days event. There may have been no fishing of the squid after all. And, perhaps, no carnival to accompany the occasion. It now seems that the most likely scenario involves squid (still in large quantities) jumping in and out of the bay by their own volition. For what purpose, I do not know. This occurrence may have gathered a small, loyal group of viewers, myself and Mr. Stills included, but it is unlikely that it was a city-sponsored event as I originally thought.

Apologetically,

Dahlia Fitzsimmons

Cyril responds, thanking Dahlia for the update. He says he has something he'd like to show her. He wants to know if she has a TV and a DVD player and, if so, can he come over?

This request comes as a surprise to Dahlia, both the enthusiasm, and the forwardness of it. She and Cyril do not know each other well. But then, maybe this is another manifestation of Cyril's Stillness—a cavalier streak in the form of a marine biology house call. And so Dahlia replies that, yes, she does have a TV and DVD player. She gives her address and nearest major cross streets.

Cyril arrives an hour later. Dahlia answers the door when the bell rings and is surprised to see how different Cyril appears outside of the laboratory. He wears no lab coat, just a faded plaid shirt, jeans, and sandals. His hair and beard look unkempt and his face, instead of cool detachment, betrays a kind of nervousness.

"I wasn't certain I had the right house," he says in a breathy way, as if he'd jogged there.

Dahlia watches Cyril's face as he peers past her inside. Something has caught his attention and is adding to his nervousness. She looks back and sees Madison standing beside the door to her bedroom, watching, her arms crossed. Dahlia ushers Cyril inside.

"Madison, this is my friend from the marine lab who I was telling you about."

Cyril nods as if eager to validate this story. He holds up a white DVD case in his left hand.

"I've got a video to show your aunt," he says.

Madison stays put and says nothing. Dahlia can't decide if the girl is being deliberately rude, or is simply unsure of how to act appropriately around men.

"You can watch it with us if you want," Cyril adds. "It's not very long."

Madison shakes her head, and when she walks past Dahlia and Cyril into the kitchen and out of sight, Cyril seems visibly relieved. Dahlia wonders if maybe Cyril isn't sure how to act around women either.

"So, uh?" Cyril holds up the DVD case.

Dahlia points him to the small TV in the corner of the living room. He turns it on, puts the disc in, and sits down on the side of the couch closest to where Dahlia has parked her chair.

"Now, what I'm wondering is," Cyril says, "did it look like this?"

He presses play on the remote and there, before Dahlia's eyes, are the squid. They leap and dive, frantic, some almost slamming into others midair. It is a strange and violent scene, hundreds of squid, tentacles pinched, eyes open, silvery bodies shuddering. The video ends after just ninety seconds. There is no sound and no credits. And yet, the action is just how Dahlia remembers it, only these squid are different—they are smaller, more angular, and darker in color.

It's odd to see, this vision from her mind projected on the television. Dahlia waits to feel the surge of emotion she associates with waking from her dream-memories. But it doesn't come. She feels hardly anything, no more than she would watching any other video that had nothing at all to do with her personally.

"Yes," Dahlia says to Cyril. "It was very much like that."

She wants to know when the video was taken. Cyril says the film was made the previous year by students at a university in Poland. The leaping squid live in the Baltic Sea. Researchers don't know why they jump like they do, but it happens every spring. There are no recorded instances of other squid doing the same thing elsewhere.

"But that doesn't mean it hasn't happened," Cyril adds.

Dahlia asks to see the video again. She hopes maybe another viewing will spark something of that Squid Days magic within her. But its images seem just as remote the second time around. While it plays, Madison emerges from the kitchen with two glasses of what appear to be pomegranate juice. She hands one to Dahlia and sets the other in front of Cyril who half-coughs a thank you.

So at least Madison is making an effort to be a good hostess, Dahlia thinks. Although she'll have to find a time to let her grandniece know that tea or coffee are the traditional beverages to offer guests, not whatever weird juice you happen to have around. She turns to suggest that a plate of cookies might also be nice, but Madison is already gone, having shuffled off to some other corner of the house.

The video has ended again, but Cyril is still looking straight ahead. He holds his juice glass in both hands, like a toddler. He seems to have sunken into the couch somewhat and it makes him look smaller, his arms and shoulders less prominent. His resemblance to Mr. Stills has all but drained out of him.

"You remind me a lot of my grandma," he says, suddenly.

Dahlia nods, unsure how to respond. She is still thinking of the squid, of Madison, of the cookie plate.

"She used a wheelchair, too, from polio."

Dahlia tells Cyril she did not have polio herself; that she was born without the use of her legs.

"Well, that's not the only reason you remind me of her."

He goes on to tell Dahlia how his grandmother was also interested in marine science, all science really, although only as an amateur pursuit. And how she'd encouraged Cyril as a boy in his own interests and was a good audience for all his childish theories and questions about the natural world, even helping him to run small experiments and collect creatures from tide pools to keep in an aquarium in his bedroom. And about how he would go over to her house every day after school to help her with little tasks she couldn't do on her own. How he misses having someone like that in his life. She passed away his senior year of high school.

Dahlia does not think any of this sounds much like her in particular.

"You remind me a bit of my little brother, Isaac," Dahlia says, not because it is true (hardly anyone ever reminds her of the inscrutable Isaac), but because the truth—*I thought you reminded me of Mr. Stills, but I was mistaken*— is too cruel, and unnecessary besides.

"Cool," Cyril says. "That's cool."

He talks for a little longer, about squid mostly. He tells Dahlia about the research he's doing for his dissertation and Dahlia thinks at first maybe he's telling her this because it relates in some way to her memory of Squid Days, but she can find little connection and decides really he's just talking to talk.

After a few more minutes, Cyril catches himself. His monologue ends abruptly and he stands to fetch his DVD from the player.

"Sorry," he says. "That's probably more information than you wanted."

Dahlia assures him, no, it was all very intriguing and she was happy to hear it. Cyril smiles at this, a look of relief.

"Hey, I'm taking a boat out tomorrow to tag market squid for my research," he says. "They're the most common species in this region. If you want, you can come with me. That way you can at least see if they're the same as the kind of squid you remember."

It's a nice offer. Again, more than Dahlia would have expected, given the nature of their relationship. Her gut instinct is to say no, thank you, that's not necessary.

But then Dahlia thinks it's maybe just what she needs—to be out on the bay, in the immediate presence of its creatures. Dahlia will see the squid in real life with her own eyes and it will fuse dream, memory, and present-day into one, and she will know for certain whatever there is about Squid Days to know.

She tells Cyril yes, she'd love to go out on the boat with him. He smiles again, says he'll e-mail her with the details.

When Cyril has gone, Madison emerges once more from her bedroom.

"What's that guy's deal, anyway?"

Dahlia asks what she means, and wonders for a moment if Madison finds Cyril attractive, and might be, in fact, interested in Cyril.

"Because he seems like a total creeper," Madison says. "You aren't planning on spending any more time with him are you?"

Dahlia tells the truth and says she is.

Dahlia spends the rest of the day wondering about the dreams that are also memories. They are so much sharper than her other dreams, so much more vivid. In them, she feels the heat of the sun-warmed sand against her body, the salt from a recently eaten fried squid snack lingering in the corners of her lips. And of course, the power of Mr. Stills' arms when he carries her. All these details, as real as the days they happened. Is it possible these dreams are a sign of some change in her body or her brain? She's worried for the past several days that other people will take the dreams as a sign she's losing her mind. But what if they really do indicate some sort of approaching decline? A stroke? Dementia? Even death? Dahlia thinks an afterlife spent on Mr. Stills' shoulders would not be so bad. Eternity as a long ride toward the water, the squid nearby, her friend holding her up.

But Dahlia dismissed these thoughts easily. She is in good health for her age. She feels fine.

She wonders, too, about the disconnect between the dream-memories and the video Cyril showed her. Granted, those weren't really her squid; they weren't even from the same continent. But they were doing the same thing, weren't they? The leaping? And yet, it meant nothing to her beyond the intellectual recognition that, yes, she had seen something like it before. Unless she hadn't, of course. Unless she'd only seen men throw squid from the bay onto the beach, or from the beach onto the bay. It occurs to her that just because the leaping dream came last, doesn't necessarily mean it's the most accurate. Or that any of the dreams were wholly and individually accurate. This makes Dahlia wonder if, even as a child, she ever really understood what Squid Days was about in the first place.

Truly, the only constant in all of the dreams is Mr. Stills. And Dahlia knows, of course, no matter where she looks, she'll never find him. Mr. Stills, the man, is long gone.

So, the more she thinks about it, the less sure she is of what she hopes to gain from a boat ride with Cyril. In fact, she has lost the little enthusiasm she first had for the trip. She wonders if she's been looking in the wrong places for Squid Days entirely. Perhaps that's why she's gained so little traction in her week of searching—why every piece of information she finds seems somehow amiss. She's been looking out—to Isaac, to Cyril, to newspapers, Web sites, ice cream parlors, and now boat rides—when she should have been looking in. She should be solving the Squid Days puzzle within herself. Whatever that might mean. Whatever shape that search might take.

After all, it's her memory, her dream. What's it got to do with anyone else? Nothing, Dahlia decides. Lonely as it may seem to admit such a thing, Squid Days has got nothing to do with anyone else at all.

But she resolves to still go. If nothing else, her presence seems to mean a great deal to Cyril. She doesn't want to appear rude or ungrateful.

The next morning, Madison helps Dahlia into the car for the drive to the marina. Dahlia is pleased by Madison's willingness to put aside valuable study time to join Dahlia for this expedition, although somewhat less pleased by Madison's reason for doing so.

"You're not going out on some boat alone with that guy," Madison said when Dahlia told her she intended to take Cyril up on his offer. "He's probably planning to murder you and feed your body to his precious squid. He'll probably make you dress up in his dead grandmother's clothes first. He'll probably make you call him Sonny Boy."

Dahlia told Madison she was being cruel. She insisted Cyril was not dangerous; he was her friend and he was doing her a favor.

In the car though, Dahlia wonders if maybe Madison senses something about the young man that Dahlia has missed.

"I'm glad you're here," Dahlia says, patting Madison's knee.

"Yeah, well, somebody has to look out for you out there on the high seas," Madison says. Then she gives Dahlia a quick wink. Such a rare and playful moment from her grandniece. It makes Dahlia want to lean over and hug the girl. But that would be too much for Madison, Dahlia knows. Instead, she decides to let Madison in on her secret.

"I wouldn't normally do this sort of thing," Dahlia says. "But it's regarding Squid Days."

"I figured. It's okay though. You've got to do what you've got to do, I guess."

"I know it seems weird, but someday you'll have something like this happen to you," Dahlia says.

"Probably not," Madison says.

Dahlia wonders which of them is correct. Does everyone have their own Squid Days? Their own Mr. Stills? Something from their past that seems so crucial and so integral to their very being, forgotten then remembered, then fractured and fissured through the maddening tricks of the human mind. And if so, what might that be for Madison? Anything at all—a particular dessert at a particular diner, a conversation with a neighbor, a broken plate or lost piece of silverware—could do the trick. There is no way to guess or to predict.

"Well, it's not a bad thing," Dahlia says, and hopes that it's true. "Just so you know. In case it does happen."

At the harbor, Madison helps Dahlia from the car and into her chair and then tells her she's going to go find a parking spot.

"Try not to get murdered before I get back," she says.

Dahlia spots Cyril nearby. He's leaning against a railing at the edge of the parking lot, looking out at the bay. Dahlia studies the back of him for a moment. He is a bit of an odd duck, she concedes. Odd, but more than that, simply different from the way Dahlia had first perceived him—from the way she first wanted to perceive him.

He's certainly picked a nice day for a boat ride though, warm with high, wispy clouds. The wheels of Dahlia's chair clatter against the rutted asphalt and Cyril turns at the sound. He greets her with a wide, genuine smile—more at ease than in her house, and more welcoming than in the lab—and begins to tell her about his plan for the afternoon, the route they will take across the bay and what he's hoping to observe from his squid once they're tagged. Dahlia nods politely.

"Well, thank you again for inviting me. And for letting Madison tag along," she says. "This is really very kind."

"I'm glad you two could come. I'm just happy to be able to help out with your Squid Days search," he says. "I really am."

Dahlia senses that is the crux of the issue for the young man. Cyril's not a "creeper" as Madison fears. And he's also not a modern-day Mr. Stills as Dahlia had first hoped. He's a lonely young man, looking for someone for whom he can be a hero. Or, if not a hero, a good helper. Dahlia remembers what Cyril said about his own grandmother. How he doesn't have anyone to help anymore. It's so strange, she thinks, the sorts of things we need from other people. Sometimes one of those needs is to be needed.

Madison appears by Dahlia's side. She announces that she's found a parking spot nearby. "So I guess we're all ready to go, or whatever," she says, kind of looking at Cyril, but not really.

Cyril nods. "There's our ride," he says.

He points to a white motorboat tied to the end of the dock. The dock is connected to the parking lot by a set of meandering wooden stairs. Dahlia knows there must be a ramp somewhere she can use—it's city property, after all—but she can't see it. She notices Madison turning her head, trying to answer the same question.

"How will I get there?" Dahlia asks.

Cyril shrugs. His big hands are wedged into the pockets of his jeans. He rocks back and forth on the balls of his feet.

"Well, I just figured…" he starts, and Dahlia knows right away what he's going to say.

It's a silly gesture, really. And an unnecessary one. Truly, there must be another way down to the dock. This isn't some action movie where Dahlia is the damsel in distress, waiting desperately to be rescued. In fact, Cyril will probably feel a little awkward about the whole thing while it's happening.

But then, Dahlia thinks, maybe in the future, when Cyril's old, his mind will flip and fracture this scene in his dreams and in his memories. And then it won't be awkward or silly or unnecessary. He'll get to play the part of the hero when he needs it. Just like Dahlia gets to be scooped up by Mr. Stills, picked out as special, shown something fantastical and wonderful in her dreams now that she needs it.

Dahlia wonders, if she could pick one part of Squid Days to make real again, what would it be? The squid? But she has seen them in Cyril's video and they meant nothing. The food and the music? It may never have existed in the first place. The companionship of her brother and parents? Who knows if they were even there, and if they were, what they thought of it. Maybe it was, to them, totally forgettable, as Isaac suggested.

No, if she could pick just one thing, it would be Mr. Stills' arms. The feeling of being held by someone strong, by someone who cared greatly for her, whatever his reason.

This is something Cyril can do for her. This is something Cyril wants to do for her. He can be those arms.

Poor Cyril, he's stammering a little now, as if he's lost his nerve. Behind him, Madison shakes her head, draws her hand in front of her neck, the universal sign for *don't encourage him*. But Dahlia wants this. She smiles up at the young man, nods her head to show her support. *Go ahead*, Dahlia thinks, willing him to stand up straight with his strong shoulders pushed back so he looks the part, so he looks more like Mr. Stills, more like Terry. Then he does, and the image is complete, and Dahlia notices how warm the sun feels on her face and how everything smells like the ocean. *Go ahead*.

"I just figured I'd carry you," Cyril says, finally. "If that's all right."

Acknowledgments

I owe tremendous thanks to the many people who have offered advice, support, and feedback for this book.

First and foremost, to my friends Michael Bell, Rosie Bartel, Melissa Huggins, Elizabeth Moore, Aaron Passman, and Maya Zeller who voluntarily took the time to read and comment on these stories in various stages of development, and to my peers from Eastern Washington University's MFA program who were forced to do so, but generally seemed to still have a good attitude about it.

To Greg Spatz, my thesis advisor at EWU, who helped me shape many of the stories in this collection, and who taught me what makes a story good in the first place.

To everyone at Featherproof Books for their diligent work on this project, but in particular to my friend and editor Jason Sommer whose enthusiasm and vision made this book far better and far weirder than anything I ever could have come up with on my own.

To Shannon Garvey for telling me about the lions and tigers of Terre Haute, Indiana.

To Cathie Johnson for pestering me to write her into a story, until I finally did.

And to my husband Scott, who I am grateful to most of all, for reasons too numerous to list here.

featherproof BOOKS

*Publishing strange and beautiful fiction and nonfiction
and post-, trans-, and inter-genre tragicomedy.*

Available at bookstores everywhere, and direct from Chicago, Illinois at
www.featherproof.com

Keep Up With The BESTSELLERS!

fp29 HISTORY IN ONE ACT: A NOVEL OF 9/11 *by William M. Arkin* $24.95

A retelling of 9/11 through the eyes of both al Qaeda and American espionage. Arkin's career (as Army intelligence analyst, human rights scholar, military consultant, and journalist) uniquely equips him to bridge these disparate worlds. And his novel answers questions no one is asking, even 20 years later: Why did it happen? Who were these people? And can we ever hope to thwart terrorism if we don't understand those who wish us harm?

fp28 TINY *by Mairead Case* $14.95

A contemporary, poetic retelling of Sophocles' *Antigone*, set in the mossy greens and foggy grays of the Pacific Northwest. Instead of two brothers who kill each other in a civil war, Tiny has a brother who kills himself after coming home from a far-away war. Using different perspectives and desires, facts from plants and history, and brass knuckles and Frankie Knuckles, *Tiny* wonders how we mourn and move, in time.

fp27 WEEPING GANG BLISS VOID YAB-YUM *by Devendra Banhart* $17.95

A poetry collection that is at turns surreal, pious, silly, and heartbreaking, but always true to its own logic, even as it creates and expands that logic as it goes. It's the most personal work Devendra Banhart has ever created... Have you ever wondered what it's like to be Devendra? Have you ever wondered what it's like to be yourself? This book.

fp26 ON THE BACK OF OUR IMAGES, VOL. I *by Luc Dardenne* $21.95

For creative people in any discipline, this book presents a master artist's mind at work, measuring sustained introspection against true and constant engagement with the world. Available for the first time in English, Luc Dardenne's diary entries as he and his brother work through their films are an extended lesson on conceptualization, collaboration, and execution.

fp25 THE SPUD *by Brielle Brilliant* $14.95

KP is the brother of a mass shooter. JD is the shooter's number 1 fan. The pair drives through rural Idaho, the physical and psychological landmarks of the violence imposing themselves on the characters and the reader. It's a flash-fiction novel for fans of *Natural Born Killers* and *Badlands*.

*fp*24 MAMMOTHER *by Zachary Schomburg* $17.95

The people of Pie Time are suffering from God's Finger, a mysterious plague that leaves its victims dead with a big hole through their chests, and in each hole is a random consumer product. With a large cast of unusual characters, each struggling with their own complex and tangled relationships to death, money, and love, *Mammother* is a fabulist's tale of how we hold on and how we let go in a rapidly growing world.

*fp*23 FROM THE INSIDE *by John Henry Timmis IV* $14.95

An autobiographical account of an adolescent's run-ins with—and attempted escapes from—the law, an abusive and uninterested family, and the Menninger Clinic sanitarium. Much like the narrators of *The Outsiders* and *Over the Edge* before him, Timmis recounts these experiences with an adolescent braggadocio, blurring intensely personal confessions and exaggerated fantasies.

*fp*21 I'M FINE, BUT YOU APPEAR TO BE SINKING *by Leyna Krow* $15.95

In this short story collection, the strange collides with the mundane: close to home and far from it, in suburban neighborhoods and rural communities, with cycling apocalypses and backyard tigers. At its core, this collection is imbued with mystery, oddity, humor, and empathy, but what it really wants to show us is that we're never really alone—most especially when we're certain that we are.

_fp_20 THE INBORN ABSOLUTE *by Robert Ryan* $60

This book collects the artist's past five years of Eastern deity paintings, mandala studies, and even an unfettered glimpse into his sketchbook. It also includes interviews with iconic performer and artist Genesis P. Orridge and legendary tattoo artist Freddy Corbin, which serve to contextualize Ryan's work and his progression as an artist.

_fp_19 MAKE X *by various artists* $30

A collection of fiction, poetry, nonfiction, conversation, and art from over a decade of Chicago-based *MAKE* magazine. Contributors include: Eula Biss, Lily Hoang, Lindsay Hunter, Dorothea Lasky, Ted Mathys, Joe Meno, Maggie Nelson, Jac Jemc, Tim Kinsella, Kathleen Rooney, Mahmoud Saeed, Tomaž Šalamun, Marvin Tate, Valeria Luiselli, and many more.

_fp_18 THE TENNESSEE HIGHWAY DEATH CHANT
by Keegan Jennings Goodman $13.95

Two teenagers are stranded in purgatory: Jenny wakes each morning, the same morning, and chronicles the events of her final day, her mind reaching back into the recesses of time, collecting a mythical past that bleeds into the details of her violent end. John drinks beer, philosophizes about the nature of reality and consciousness, and hurtles his Firebird Trans Am into the darkness beyond the headlights.

*fp*17 SUNSHINE ON AN OPEN TOMB *by Tim Kinsella*
$16.95

It's fall 1988—the advent of the 24-hour news cycle—and the brooding runt of an American political dynasty is of interest to The Media when his father is about to be appointed Prez. When The Family relocates him to their secret, shape-shifting estate, this runt is forced to confront an impossible love triangle while he sets to work on his revenge.

*fp*16 ERRATIC FIRE, ERRATIC PASSION *by Jeff Parker & Pasha Malla* $14.95

The content of postgame interviews and sports chatter is often meaningless, if not insufferable. But some athletes transcend lame clichés and rote patter, using language in surprising, funny, and insightful ways. This book of "found" poems uses athletes' own words to celebrate those rare moments, with an introduction by award-winning sports writer Bethlehem Shoals.

JNR170.3 ALL OVER AND OVER *by Tim Kinsella* $14.95

In 2003, living on constant tour through the dark days of the dawn of The War on Terror, Joan of Arc decided to regroup as a political hardcore band: Make Believe. For the next few years they maintained a grueling schedule. These are Kinsella's journals of their final, full U.S. tour—when he had to admit that the cost-benefit ratio of this lifestyle had toppled and he needed to stop.

fp13 THE MINUS TIMES COLLECTED: TWENTY YEARS / THIRTY ISSUES (1992–2012) *edited by Hunter Kennedy* $16.95

Banged out on a 1922 Underwood typewriter, this 'zine began as an open letter to strangers and fellow misfits then grew into a breeding ground for the next generation of American fiction. Featuring Sam Lipsyte, Wells Tower, David Eggers, Dan Clowes, Barry Hannah, a yet-to-be-famous Stephen Colbert, and many more, with an introduction by Patrick DeWitt.

fp12 THE KARAOKE SINGER'S GUIDE TO SELF-DEFENSE *by Tim Kinsella* $14.95

Reunited for a funeral, a family finds dissonance in the fragments of their shared memories: a thoughtful dancer back at her bar, a bitter father working in a toothpaste factory, and a fist-fight addict struggling to keep his nose clean. Across town, a boy is locked up in a delusional man's home, and a teenage runaway looks for a new life in a strip club. Cruelty is a given. Karaoke is every Thursday.

fp11 THE UNIVERSE IN MINIATURE IN MINIATURE *by Patrick Somerville* $14.95

In this genre-busting book of short stories we find a Chicago man who is bequeathed a supernatural helmet that allows him to experience the inner worlds of those around him; we peer into the mind of an art student grappling with ennui; we telescope out to the story of idiot extraterrestrials struggling to pilot a complicated spaceship; and we follow a retired mercenary as he tries to save his marriage and questions his life abroad.

9 781943 888085